A NEW LIFE

"What are we going to do about furniture, Mom?" Robbie asked Susan.

"We'll check the newspaper for used pieces. Until I get a job, we'll have to be really careful."

"I understand." Robbie went and retrieved the newspaper they'd bought earlier that morning. "What do I look under?"

"Used furniture," Susan called from the bedroom, where she'd gone with the hanging bag. She unzipped the bag and took out her dresses and hung them on the pole in the narrow closet. She placed her boxes of shoes on the floor. She stood there staring at the empty floor.

If she'd been catapulted to another planet, Susan couldn't have felt any more out of touch with her surroundings. What was she doing here? Was this all worth it? How could she ask Robbie to give up his life, when it was her life that needed changing? Her hand flew to her throat as she felt icy fingers of fear begin to choke her.

She quickly shut the closet door and realized there was a full-length mirror on the other side. She stared at her reflection. She touched her cheek. *He could have broken it. Maybe next time he would have. Maybe next time he would not have stopped. What if the next time became another next time until you were dead, Susan? Then what would Robbie do?*

She placed her hands on the mirror and lowered her forehead to the glass. *You did the right thing. You did the right thing.*

Other *Leisure* books by Catherine Lanigan:
SEDUCED

BECOMING

Catherine Lanigan

LEISURE BOOKS NEW YORK CITY

This book is dedicated to the administration, staff and personnel of STAR OF HOPE MISSION in Houston, Texas, and to all the volunteers and kindhearted souls who give their time and emotions to women's shelters across the nation. With their guiding light for so many troubled families, this world is truly the brightest home in the universe.

A LEISURE BOOK®

June 1997

Published by

Dorchester Publishing Co., Inc.
276 Fifth Avenue
New York, NY 10001

Copyright © 1997 by Catherine Lanigan

Printed in the United States of America.

BECOMING

Chapter One

New Orleans, June 1996

Susan felt a rage-packed fist hit her jaw. She heard an odd-sounding crunch before she felt the pain and was unsure whether the sound had come from her jawbone or the cracking of his fingers. She prayed it was the latter. She wanted him to hurt as much as she was . . . or more. Before Jim had a chance to land a second blow from his left hand to her right cheek she ducked and scrambled out of his line of vision. Jim was drunk and she knew from past experience that when he was this far gone he'd never be able to keep up with her quick moves. She dodged to the right and whirled around behind him. She didn't dare kick him or land a blow because he would only become more angry. What she wanted was to exhaust him.

The sharp, jabbing pain in her jaw had radiated to include what felt like half her face, but she couldn't waste a split second thinking about it or she would lose her advantage over him.

Jim grabbed her arm. "You bitch!" He squeezed very hard on the fleshy underside of her arm. Susan winced and tried to break free, but Jim only tightened his grip. She screamed.

"Awww! Let me go!"

Suddenly Susan became terrified that her cries would wake Robbie, her seven-year-old son, who was sleeping in the first bedroom down the hall. She closed her mouth and glared at Jim.

"That's right. That's right. You don't want to wake Robbie. Precious Robbie. You'd do anything for him, wouldn'tcha? But you won't for me, huh? Isn't that about the size of it?"

"Let me go, Jim." She struggled against him, forcing herself to forget that he was her husband, the man she loved and who was supposed to love her. Jim wasn't Jim anymore.

"No. I want you to listen to me."

"I'll listen when you're sober."

"You don't listen to me then, either. Nobody does. Not you. Not your precious Robbie—"

"He's your son, too," Susan tried to reason with him. She made a special effort to keep her voice soothing and clear of the pain she felt from her jaw and in her heart.

"You claim. Guess I'll never really know." He dug his emotional knife in deep for the kill, yet the thought caused him to falter for a half moment. The glitch in time gave Susan the break she needed. She wrenched free of his grasp and dodged his next attack when he dove toward her with the full force of his body.

Susan was taking no chances. She quickly turned to the right and stuck her leg directly across his path, tripping him.

Jim went sailing toward the hardwood floor and landed hard, as if he'd passed out cold in midair. His head banged on the floor with a sickening thud.

Becoming

Susan counted to three before she approached Jim's body. She didn't care if he was dead. She needed to be certain he wasn't still awake and simply waiting to pounce on her again. She stood cautiously next to his still body. She kicked him lightly in the ribs. She felt like one of those heroines in a movie thriller when the audience is screaming, "Don't go near him! He's still alive! Stay away! Stay away!"

Susan heeded her own inner voice and quickly stepped over him and went straight to her bedroom.

Finally the night had come when she could execute her plan. She went to her bedroom and from under the bed pulled out four pieces of brand-new soft collapsible luggage still in the shopping bag from WalMart. She rolled up the WalMart bag and shoved it under the belt in her jeans for later use. She quickly opened all her drawers in the bureau and began carefully filling the suitcases. Everything fit nicely and neatly, just as she'd thought.

For six months Susan Kidd had thought of nothing else except how she would escape from Jim. The question of *if* she should leave Jim had been settled in her mind after Christmas last year, when Jim had hit her for the first time. Her eye was so badly blackened, she'd spent nearly the entire month of January indoors. She knew that if he'd crossed the line once, he would surely beat her again. That January she had devised her plan and begun to make subtle alterations in the way she kept house.

Susan had placed in the first bureau drawer all the things she would need when she ran away: passport, credit cards, savings bonds, cash—it was only three hundred dollars she'd saved from her grocery money, but still cash. One pair of gold hoop earrings, a ruby dinner ring her parents had given her on her eighteenth birthday, and her small diamond engagement ring had all been carefully placed inside a blue drawstring cloth bag with the Seagram's Royal Crown logo embroidered on the front. The Kidds owned many of these bags, indiscreet testimony to the extent of Jim's drinking these days. Susan had used them to store everything from Robbie's marbles to Jim's cuff links. Jim would never miss this one. She knew her jewelry would bring her no more than a few hundred dollars at a pawn shop, but it was all she had.

In the second drawer were neat rows of panties, socks, hose, bras, slips, and two nightgowns. She carefully placed them in the nylon duffel bag. In the next drawer were jeans, sweatshirts, T-shirts, and sweaters, all in perfect piles ready to be packed. Out of each drawer Susan took only half the items, then rearranged the remainder so that when she finished the drawers looked as if they'd never been touched.

Susan barely needed to think since she had long ago arranged these drawers. When she opened the closet she went to the back, where she had packed two boxes with the shoes she would take. She disturbed nothing on her shoe rack. She put the boxes in the suitcase. Toward the back of the closet, Susan had preselected a group of dresses that were still twist-tied together and hanging in an ordinary cleaner's bag. She took the dresses and put them in her hanging bag, along with a brand-new raincoat that still bore a price tag. She returned to the closet and slid the remaining hangers down the closet pole to eliminate the small gap in the rear.

Quickly, she went to the bathroom and carefully selected brown eyeshadow, mascara, a bottle of liquid makeup, one blush, one makeup brush, a moisturizer, and a lipstick. She painstakingly made certain her shelves looked absolutely normal. She left her used blue toothbrush and instead took one from a stack of new toothbrushes she kept on hand.

Susan took the filled suitcases down the hall, walking over Jim, who was still out cold on the living-room floor, through the kitchen and into the garage. She opened the trunk of her four-year-old blue Taurus and placed the bags in the trunk.

Retracing her steps, Susan went back into the house, took

the WalMart bag from under her belt, and silently entered Robbie's room.

"Thank God he's still asleep," she muttered to herself as she set about her task. She placed a stuffed Barney that Robbie had owned for three years and whose fuzzy cheek was worn thin from constant nuzzling, into the bag. A Dr. Seuss book, a Bible stories book, a solar-powered calculator Robbie carried everywhere, his GameBoy and a dozen games. Inside Robbie's closet, Susan had prepacked a plastic bag with a week's wardrobe for her son. She grabbed his robe, Mickey Mouse slippers, jacket, a Saints baseball cap, and his rain gear, then stuffed everything into the WalMart bag. She quietly left the room and put both bags in the trunk of the car.

She opened the garage door, put the car in neutral, and let it roll silently out of the garage and onto the driveway. She went back into the house and grabbed her purse from the desk in the kitchen, then went to Robbie's room.

She took one last look around the room with its sky blue ceiling studded with the stars and planets she had lovingly painted herself. God, how she remembered the afternoons she had spent with five-year-old Robbie, planning the exact placement of every star. They had had such dreams for a joyous future back then. For the first time that night her emotions broke through and nearly immobilized her. Huge tears filled her eyes, nearly blinding her to her goal of escape. What if she was wrong? How would the world judge her? She should stand by her man, her friends had told her; but then, she'd never told anyone about the abuse—mental or physical. Susan had kept her dark realities from her family, her friends, and even sheltered Jim from the truth about himself. She'd been a good wife, all right. Too good.

Her eye caught Robbie's wooden toy box, which Jim had made himself for Robbie's second birthday. For a short time, only a few months, when Robbie had been constantly ill with high fevers from strep throat, Jim had rallied to Robbie's aid.

The night before Robbie's birthday Susan had walked the floor for four and a half hours with a screaming, sick little boy. Jim had slept through most of it, but by three in the morning he took over and rocked Robbie till dawn, when the fever miraculously broke. It was enough of a reprieve for Susan to rest and gather her strength again. That birthday, Susan's parents had stopped by for cake and ice cream, and Jim had proudly shown off the toy box, as if he was stunned at his own abilities.

Susan could hear the echoes of their laughter that day still reverberating in this room. She nearly succumbed to her memories, but mingled among the good times were the ethers of Jim's castigations. This was her home, damn it. She should feel safe here, protected, and she wasn't.

This house, this life with Jim, had turned into a nightmare, and Susan couldn't understand where or why it had gone awry. Her home had become hell.

She touched the snowy blond hair on her son's head and, as always, was moved by the miracle that God had given her in Robbie. She was amazed that this beautiful creature, this person so full of life, love, and joy, had been born from her body. It was awesome. Yet Jim didn't think so.

Robbie yawned. "Mommy?"

"Come on, pumpkin." Susan put her arms around Robbie and lifted him. He was still a frail-looking child, long and thin, blue-eyed and beautiful. It was his beauty and fragility that frightened Jim sometimes, she knew. Susan was always fearful that Jim would call Robbie names, ever since last summer, when she'd first heard him call Robbie a sissy for preferring the computer to football.

Jim had played football for Tulane University when they'd met. He was the campus star his senior year, when Susan had been pledging sororities. Jim belonged to Phi Kappa Psi and, as president of the fraternity, he was assisting the president of Kappa Alpha Theta, Julie Menton, with a reception for the new pledges. Susan had arrived an hour early to the reception because her invitation had stated the wrong time. Jim had been in the process of spiking the punch when Susan walked up.

"Hi," she said, nearly startling Jim out of his dark blue sport coat and tan slacks.

He quickly stashed the bottle of vodka under the pink linen–skirted table. "Hi."

"Do you . . . work here, or are you a member?" she teased.

"I—yi—yi—yi . . . Are you the most gorgeous thing I've ever seen or what?" He placed his hands on the table and leaned very close to her.

"I wouldn't know." Susan glanced down and turned her head away, letting her blond curls cover her blushing cheeks. Susan was used to compliments, but this handsome boy was nearly leaping over the table at her.

"You . . . you're blushing. Nobody blushes anymore."

"Sorry." She smiled. *"It's a genetic thing. I always do that when I'm embarrassed."*

Jim came around from behind the table. "And I'm embarrassing you. That's good. It's a reaction. Reaction is good."

"It is? How?"

"It shows I have your attention."

As the years passed, Susan had thought how prophetic Jim's first words to her had been. Everything Jim did was to gain attention, and with him, she was perpetually a reactive woman. He drank. She pleaded and begged him to stop. He drank more. She nagged, she screamed, she pouted, she cajoled, she acquiesced. She did everything. This time she was leaving.

*   *   *

I should have seen it coming. The signs . . . they were there back in college, weren't they? He was always an attention getter . . . the star of the football team; the president of his fraternity and the vice-president of Panhellenic. She mentally reviewed her past again. When Jim went into his first job, with Metro Media Advertising, a position Susan's father, Bart Beaulieu, had arranged for him, Jim wasn't satisfied until the title behind his name said "manager." And yet everyone, especially Susan's parents, knew that he was simply an apprentice.

Jim was charming and effusive with praise and compliments to people whom he felt he needed to build his client list. Jim took his clients to posh Bourbon Street restaurants, haggled with the scalpers for prime Saints football tickets, and made certain his clients received ostentatious gourmet baskets filled with liquor, food, and more liquor during the holidays each year. Jim quickly rose to the top in his firm. The fact that he hadn't created an original advertising campaign for a single client never bothered Jim. He simply stole another idea from one of the young college interns the firm employed when the workload was heavy. Jim made certain there were plenty of happy clients and the firm rewarded Jim with a promotion to sales director, a position that allowed him a longer leash to wine and dine clients.

The off shoot of Jim's rise in power and recognition within Metro Media Advertising was that Jim became an alcoholic.

Susan had discovered the truth over five years earlier, when the three of them had traveled to Horsehoe Bend, Arkansas, for a four-day vacation. Douglas Martin, the president of the firm, had personally suggested that Jim take some time off. Susan hadn't paid much attention to the request until their drive to Arkansas, when they'd stopped for dinner. Robbie was two and a half years old, tired, bored with driving, and hungry. Susan was famished, but Jim wouldn't stop to eat until he found a restaurant where he could have a beer with

14

his hamburger. They'd driven until eight-thirty, by which time Susan was suffering from a headache, Robbie had fallen asleep, and Jim was cursing every crossroads in Texarkana because nothing was open where he could get a beer.

Jim drank three beers that night. The next morning, at ten-thirty, he ordered a Bloody Mary. He had a martini with a tuna fish sandwich for lunch and four more beers by the pool during the afternoon. At five-thirty Susan was about to bathe for dinner when Jim walked out of the bathroom, fully dressed in a suit. "I think I'll go down to the bar and wait for you."

"I think you've had enough to drink for one day."

Jim looked at Susan as if she were crazy. "I'm only having a cocktail."

"Just one?"

"Who cares if I have more than one?"

"I do," she said, firmly placing her hands on her hips.

Jim grabbed her wrist and yanked on her arm . . . hard. "Don't play high and mighty with me. I'll do anything I damn well please. If you're not coming to dinner, then say so." He pulled on her arm again as she slid her other arm down to her side.

Susan looked over at Robbie, who was sitting in a huge seafoam green barrel-shaped chair at the table by the window, playing with a new set of Lincoln Logs. She watched as Robbie kept his eyes on his work and his head down, as if he was oblivious to the tension around him, but Susan spied the almost imperceptible pause as Robbie was about to place a red wooden chimney on the green slatted roof he'd just made. "My God," she thought to herself, "Robbie knows."

Susan knew better than to show him the defiance she felt. "I'll be there."

"Bring him," Jim said stiffly and left the room.

Robbie jumped when the door slammed. He looked over at Susan with huge blue eyes filled with confusion and fear.

Robbie didn't know what was wrong, but he knew something wasn't right. "Is Daddy mad at me?"

Susan rushed to reassure him. She put her arms around his neck. "Heavens no, darlin'. He's just got a lot on his mind. His work is very difficult these days, so I guess the best thing for us to do is be patient with him. Can you do that?"

"Sure, Mommy. I can cheer him up." He smiled and hugged her back.

As the days and weeks passed, Jim was busier than ever. He seldom came home for dinner, leaving Susan to feed Robbie and care for him herself. Susan took care of the house, mowed the lawn, planted the shrubs, fixed the screens, and packed Jim's shirts for another "road" trip. They said goodbye on Mondays and hello late Friday nights.

Jim spent virtually no time with his son. When Robbie was a baby Jim had felt threatened by the dependency of an infant. When he was a preschooler Jim felt Robbie had nothing to say other than idle child's prattle. Once Robbie was in first grade Jim realized they could at least play catch and pass a football back and forth, but Robbie had little interest in sports other than swimming and biking. Robbie had replaced his father with video games and the computer, and Jim felt the situation was comfortable for them both.

It wasn't until this last night in her home, as she carried her young son to the car, that Susan Kidd faced the darkest of her realities. Jim had never wanted Robbie, and he blamed Susan and to some degree Robbie himself for all the "ills" in his life.

Susan put Robbie in the front passenger seat of the car, shut the door, and raced around to her side of the car and got in.

Quietly, she let the car roll down the drive and, once into the street, started the ignition and drove away.

Susan never looked back at the pretty house she'd spent eight years decorating, tending, and living in. She wouldn't allow herself to look at the elm tree she'd planted two weeks after Robbie was born, nor the azalea garden she and her mother had planted together. She didn't want to think of what she was giving up. She thought solely of freedom.

They drove across the canal and then turned onto Cleary and drove north to Veteran's Highway. By the time they were two blocks away from the house Robbie was awake.

Robbie fastened his seat belt like a pro, crossed his arms over his chest, and looked straight at his mother. "We're running away from Daddy, aren't we, Mommy?"

In all her planning, her dreams, the well-thought-out details, not once had she thought about how she would explain this to Robbie. They had always been so psychically linked, she had simply assumed he would know what she was doing. She had been right.

"Yes."

"It's because he hit you."

"How . . . how did you know that?"

"Your eye is red and your cheek is all swelled up."

Susan immediately yanked on the rearview mirror and looked at her face. God, she'd forgotten he'd hit her. Forgotten the pain. She remembered the crunching sound she'd heard when his fist made contact with her face. She moved her jaw from left to right, up and down. No, it wasn't broken, thank God. But it did hurt like hell.

There were tears in Robbie's eyes. "Why did Daddy hit you?"

"It's okay, pumpkin."

"No, it's not. It's wrong to hit somebody you love."

"That's right, Robbie. I meant it's okay, because we're never going back there again. We're not going to live with Daddy anymore."

"Promise?" Robbie's voice was filled with relief.

"Yes," she said with firm determination as she sped down Vet's Highway.

"But, when he sees we're gone he'll come looking for us and make us go back."

Susan was amazed that Robbie knew Jim's behavior nearly as well as she. "No he won't. I fixed it."

Robbie looked at his mother quizzically. "How?"

Susan checked the rearview mirror to make very certain she didn't see Jim's steel gray Mercedes behind her. "He knows we're gone, but I took only a few of our things. I made it look like we *would* be coming back, so that he won't think to look farther than New Orleans for us."

"You tricked him?"

"Yes. And I know what I told you before about tricking people, but this time it's okay."

Robbie released some slack on his seat belt and pushed his elbows against the back of the seat to raise himself up for a better view of the highway. "Then we aren't going to Gramma's?" Robbie asked as they drove up the street that would take them to the elegant lakefront home of Susan's parents.

"No. Not to Mother's. That's the first place Daddy would look." *And I don't know how to tell them the truth. I've spent so much time and energy covering Jim's drinking. Cleaning up his messes. Making fantasy out of reality. They would never believe me. They would tell me to go back and God, I don't know how I could face the shame.* How many times had her mother, Annette, told her how proud she was of Susan and what a good homemaker she'd become? Annette had continually extolled the virtues of being a good wife and mother, "when so many young girls get divorced at the drop of a hat," as she said. "Thank God there has never, ever, been a divorce in the Beaulieu family." According to Annette Beaulieu, divorce was the scourge of the earth and responsible for nearly every evil one could name.

God, oh, God. How could I have made such a mess of things?

"That was good thinking not to go to Gramma's, Mommy."

"Thanks, pumpkin." She smiled at her son, not wanting him to know that her fears fluttered in her brain like bats in a cage.

"You're welcome." Robbie smiled back and reached out his hand to Susan. How odd it was that Robbie trusted her implicitly. He didn't trust Jim. He was judicious with his friendships and didn't like many children. For the most part Robbie thought children were silly little people who played stupid games, for whom he had little time. Susan had always thought that Robbie was one of those souls who reincarnated much too quickly and had not quite figured out they had been reborn again. Oftentimes, Robbie reminded her of an old man in a child's body, because he became so easily frustrated during those years when he tried to walk and talk. Once he learned to put his sentences together Robbie had never shut up. His vocabulary was extensive and, because of "Sesame Street," he could speak broken Spanish. Robbie never told his father that he thought football and team sports were a stupid waste of time and energy better spent on more important things. But he told Susan. Robbie wasn't afraid of being hurt, as Jim had accused him, nor was he a sissy; Robbie simply thought he should be spending his time reading about geography or history or famous people.

Robbie was a little man, all right, Susan thought as she looked at his outstretched hand and took it. His little hand fit so perfectly in her palm. She squeezed it tight, and her heart nearly burst with love for him.

She would hold on to Robbie, she thought. For Robbie . . . she must hold on.

Chapter Two

They slept in the car that night just south of Baton Rouge in a cluster of trees just off Louisiana State 12 highway. Susan had avoided the interstate, believing that if Jim did try to follow her, he'd think it the most natural route. By choosing smaller roads she figured she would more easily evade him.

It was after midnight when Susan's energy seemed to drain out of her completely. The adrenaline she'd earlier felt rushing through her body, pushing her to flee, was gone. Robbie had managed to stay awake for nearly two and a half hours, but he, too, was exhausted.

Susan was awakened by a bright light shining in her eyes. Her muscles were stiff when she sat upright and squinted at the dawn. She blinked and realized this wasn't sunlight.

He was tall, thin, darkly dressed, and carried a gun. "What are you doing here?" he asked through the closed window.

"Sleeping," she said, fear nearly strangling her response. She put up her hand to her eyes to deflect the offensive light.

"Sorry," he said and snapped off the flashlight. He bent

down to the window. That was when Susan saw the badge on his shirt, the nightstick in his belt, and the brown state trooper hat he wore.

She rolled down the window.

Susan let out a sigh of relief and then immediately checked herself. What if Jim had called the police? God! Were they after her already? Wasn't it customary to wait twenty-four hours before reporting a missing person? Susan had counted on those twenty-four hours. She needed every one of them, and now she'd wasted valuable time . . . sleeping. She was a fool.

"Is there something wrong, Officer?"

"You tell me."

"I thought it the better part of wisdom to pull off the road rather than fall asleep at the wheel and kill us. And possibly somebody else, too."

"You're right." He leaned into the window and saw Robbie sleeping next to Susan. "But I passed by here an hour ago and there was no one here. It's just as dangerous to be alone like you are. You don't know who might stop."

"Thank God it was you."

"You might say that. Let me see your driver's license."

"What for?"

"I want to make a record of where you live."

Susan braced herself. She couldn't let him know. Then it would go on the computers at the State Police's central office, and Jim could easily track her down. She had to think quickly.

"I live in Metairie. My mother is in Baton Rouge, and I got a call that she was taken ill. My son and I are on our way there now to see her. I just didn't realize how tired I was. As you said, I wasn't here an hour ago. I guess we'd better be on our way."

"Not so fast," he said gruffly. "Wait here," he said and walked away back toward his car.

Susan watched the officer go to his car, open the door, and

search the seat for something. "Please God, don't let him call me in."

Just then Robbie awakened. "What is it, Mommy? Is something wrong?"

"No, darlin'. It's fine. Just fine."

"Why are we stopping?"

"I just had to take a little nap is all." She smoothed his hair with her hand. His face was swollen from sleep in the way that all children's faces do because they sleep so deeply and hard. Sleep of the innocent, she thought as she leaned over and kissed his cheek.

"Here you go, ma'am," the officer said.

Susan straightened and was about to lash out at the man for giving her a ticket when she'd done nothing wrong. She turned her head to face him and found herself looking at a plastic mug with brown lettering stating LOUISIANA'S FINEST.

"What's this?"

"Coffee. I thought you could use some, and I don't mind sharing."

Susan smiled at him. "But it's your mug."

"It's okay. You keep it. I've got another." He leaned down and looked at Robbie. "You take care of your mother, now, ya hear?" He looked back at Susan. "I hope your mother is all right."

"She'll be fine. I'm sure of it," Susan said, taking the coffee mug and sipping it. The coffee was hot and very good.

The officer walked away. As he got into his car, Susan started the ignition, turned on the lights, and pulled out of the graveled clearing.

"Buckle up, Robbie," she said and pulled onto the highway. She noticed that the officer didn't follow her, and for that she was also grateful to him.

Officer Mulday picked up his receiver and spoke to the dispatcher on the other end. "It was nothin', Gary, just some

22

young woman and her son. She gave me a cock-and-bull story about going to see her sick mother. She had a shiner you wouldn't believe. Pretty girl, too. I hope she makes it.''

Gary, the dispatcher on the other end, said, ''Ha! Likely chance she'll go back to the son of a bitch who beat her. They all do.''

''Not all, Gary. My sister didn't and she's doin' fine. Jes' fine.''

''Yeah, but she had you.''

''Yep. She did. She was luckier than most.'' Officer Mulday filled a styrofoam cup with coffee from his Thermos. ''Well, I hope she doesn't do another fool thing like sleepin' on the side of the road. I'm lucky I found her still alive. Doesn't she ever read the papers about this neck of the woods? Shit.''

Gary, on the other end, grumbled. ''Ten four.''

''Out.''

Officer Mulday drove to the break in the meridian and sped down Louisiana State Highway 12, his eyes searching the night for people in trouble.

Susan traded her Taurus to a Baton Rouge used-car dealer thirty-five minutes after the man opened his doors for business. Because this had been part of her plan, several weeks earlier Susan had found the title on her car and had talked Jim into putting the car solely in her name. She made an issue of the fact that he had a fifty-thousand-dollar car and the Blue Book value on her car was only seven thousand dollars. She had been fortunate enough to catch him at a time when he was preoccupied with closing with a very important client, so he had quickly scribbled his name on the necessary papers and forms she'd procured from the license bureau and tax assessor's offices.

Susan traded down to a 1990 Cutlass Supreme with ninety thousand miles on it and took three thousand dollars in a cashier's check. She signed her name to all the necessary papers knowing that she would never have the car long enough to receive the valid plates. For her address she gave the address of a former sorority sister, Mary Anderson, who now lived with her husband in Baton Rouge. She chuckled to herself when she thought about how surprised Mary would be when she received papers regarding license plates for a car she'd never bought. Poignantly, she wondered if Mary was happy . . . was Don good to her? She hadn't spoken to Mary in years, which was Susan's fault, because Susan had isolated herself from her friends once she'd realized Jim was an alcoholic. She hoped Jim had forgotten about Mary. Susan didn't want Mary to be subjected to Jim's questions or harrassment when he came looking for her.

Robbie helped Susan unload their things from the Taurus into the "new" car.

"Gees, Mommy. Couldn't you buy a better car than this?" Robbie looked at the pitted and sun-faded brown car with its creaky doors. He glanced back over the lot of cars. "How about that white Trans Am? I like sports cars."

"I bought the ugliest car he had—"

"*I know!*" Robbie interrupted with a huff of indignation.

"—for a reason. I wanted the cash difference."

Robbie's head whirled around to face his mother as she put the last two suitcases in the trunk. "He gave you money?"

"Yes. A lot of money for us to start our new life."

Robbie puffed out his chest proudly and then patted her on the shoulder. "That was smart, Mommy."

Susan smiled broadly as she closed the trunk. "Thanks."

"You're welcome," he replied. He hopped into the car and buckled his seat belt.

As she checked both ways for oncoming traffic, she said to Robbie, "Don't worry about the car. We won't have it long. I intend to sell it today."

"Whoa! That's pretty quick."

"I have to be quick." She checked her watch. It was nearly nine o'clock. As she drove out of Baton Rouge she could feel Jim's breath on the back of her neck.

Jim awoke to the sound of the ringing telephone. His brain felt like the insides of a gravel pit. His thought patterns were craggy and disjointed. "Whaaa?"

The telephone rang again.

He pushed himself up from the floor, wondering what in the hell he was doing there and not in bed. His body ached all over.

"Jesus, I really tied one on last night."

The telephone rang a third time.

Jim stood and clumped his way to the kitchen, picked up the receiver from the wall phone, and said, "Hello?"

"Jim, where the hell are you?" Barry Whitestone said.

"Uh, I . . . I'm just out the door. Why? What's going on?"

"What's going on? The Yamazaki people are here, dammit, and you have all our presentation materials in your Benz. Shit . . . Jim. Are you still drunk?"

"Me? No way."

"Well, you had an awful lot last night at Commander's Palace."

Jim laughed. "Yeah, I did. Who would have guessed those little Japs could drink so much? I swear to God, they were stone sober when I left."

"Well, they're real goddamn sober now and want to see our stuff. I told them you had car trouble."

"Good thinking. I'll be there in fifteen minutes."

"Fifteen, but I don't think I can stall them any more," Barry said and hung up.

"Shit." Jim looked down at his rumpled clothes. Jesus. He didn't even remember last night. He raced down the hall to the bedroom and, as he did, his head pounded like the inside of a rap singer's ghetto blaster. He tore off his tie, shirt, and suit pants. He didn't bother to shower, but wetted his hair down with water and ran a quick razor over his scruffy beard. He quickly put on a freshly laundered shirt, which Susan had hung neatly on his side of the walk-in closet, sans the cleaner's bag. It was an order he'd given her because he detested plastic bags that never seemed to come off his shirts, especially when he was in a hurry. He took out a freshly cleaned worsted wool suit and laid it on the made bed. As he was tying his tie and routing in his drawer for the right pair of socks, he glanced back at the smooth coverlet on the bed and realized that Susan had started her day early.

He also realized that Susan had not seen to it that he made it to bed last night. Why, she'd let him stay on the living-room floor, where he'd obviously passed out. What the hell was the matter with her these days?

He stepped into his slacks, pulled on designer socks, and shoved his feet into his new Italian loafers. God, how he loved fine clothes. Susan had grown up with such things and, therefore, he believed she didn't have the same sense of appreciation for the beautiful appointments of life as he did.

Jim found a bottle of B-12s in the medicine cabinet, poured a half dozen tablets into his palm and, along with two aspirin, downed the entire handful with a huge glass of water. He could almost feel the rush of blood to his brain. Instant revitalization. That's what he needed with his Japanese clients.

Jim raced down the hall, not even glancing into Robbie's room. He grabbed his suitcase, which was still sitting by the front door where he'd left it, he guessed. As he locked the door he said a silent prayer that he'd close this deal today. It was the most important thing in his life.

Chapter Three

Susan drove north to Alexandria, Louisiana, where she sold the Cutlass for fifteen hundred dollars, now knowing that the car dealer in Baton Rouge had bilked her out of another fifteen hundred dollars she should have made on the sale of the Taurus. However, Susan thought, it was worth fifteen hundred dollars to throw Jim off her track. Purposefully, she had driven north, so that Jim might think she was on her way to St. Louis, where her good friend, Jamie Wilkins, lived. Jamie and her husband, Nate, had visited Susan and Jim in New Orleans nearly every year for the past eight years, and the two women regularly corresponded.

Just thinking about Jamie and all the fun times they'd had in the past chipped away at Susan's determination. Susan wouldn't be able to call Jamie and talk endlessly about gardening, parties, the house, and the kids the way they always had, because Jamie knew Susan well enough to detect even the slightest lie. Jamie was another valuable piece of her life with Jim she was being forced to abandon.

With each mile she passed the weight of Susan's decision pressed in on her. Even though she was putting distance between herself and Jim, she was also cutting herself off from all that was good about her life in New Orleans.

The car dealer had arranged for one of his salesmen to drive Susan, Robbie, and their belongings to the bus terminal. Susan pretended there were no tears in her eyes as she walked up to the counter to buy a pair of tickets, but she had a much more difficult time erasing the vision of her mother's face that seemed to loom before her.

"Two tickets to St. Louis, please," Susan told the ticket agent.

The fat young woman handed Susan two tickets, took her cash, and gave Susan the proper change. Susan turned around wearily in time to see Robbie walking away from the drinking fountain and coming toward her, his WalMart bag in tow, wiping his mouth with his sleeve.

"What have I done to my little boy?" she thought to herself. "I'm leaving all my friends behind, but so is he. He's had to leave his school, his friends, his grandparents, and his father, but he hasn't complained once."

Robbie took Susan's hand. "Come on, Mommy. Let's sit down till the bus gets here. You look tired."

Susan rolled her eyes to keep the tears at bay. How could God have given her such an angel? What made her so lucky? "I am tired."

They sat in scratched gold and avocado green plastic chairs across from a young girl in jeans, cowboy boots, and a bandanna-print halter top. She looked to be no more than sixteen herself, yet she had what looked to be a two-year-old daughter and a four-year-old little boy with her. The girl lit a cigarette and let it dangle from her bottom lip as she changed the disposable diaper on her daughter. The little boy was making a tremendous racket, banging the chairs with a plastic sword and saying he was Sir Galahad.

28

"Stop that, Jason!" the girl yelled at her son. "Stop it right this instant or I'll smack you again."

Jason paid no attention to his mother, obviously assuming that while his mother was occupied with his sister, he could do as he pleased.

Suddenly the girl uprighted her daughter into the chair and, with the lightning speed of a rattlesnake striking prey, her arm lashed out and she slapped Jason's shoulder hard. Susan thought she could have dislocated it.

Susan winced. Robbie shuddered and instantly grabbed his mother's arm for protection.

"Goddamn it, Jason. I've got a frickin' headache. Now knock it off!"

The noise Jason made from the painful blow was twice as loud as the noise he'd made with his sword. The young girl grabbed Jason by his upper arms and shook him. She stuck her face right next to his and growled at him. "Make one more sound and you're gonna regret it."

Jason instantly quieted and stood stock still in front of his mother.

Susan blinked and mentally rewound the scene in her head. Why hadn't she seen it before? That girl grabbed her young son in exactly the same manner Jim always grabbed her. God! And how she hated the way he would pinch the underside flesh, often leaving bruises no one would ever see. Was that how Jim learned to do those things to her? From his mother? Was that how it started? And where did she learn it? From her mother before that? And before that?

Questions without answers, important questions, thundered through Susan's head like an avalanche. Suddenly the bus pulled into the station. Passengers rose from their seats. The loudspeaker was turned on and a creaky man's voice began announcing arrivals and departures. Susan's thoughts got lost in the flood of hustle and bustle. She reminded herself that she must evaluate this new insight of hers when she had the time. When she wasn't so frantic; when each right move wasn't so very important to her plan.

Susan and Robbie watched while the bus driver placed their bags in the luggage compartment in the belly of the bus. Robbie carried his WalMart bag with him and chose their seats near the back, close to the bathroom. Robbie sat next to the window.

The bus driver came down the aisle, punching everyone's ticket, keeping the yellow portion for himself, and handing back the pink portion to each passenger. When he finished he handed the tickets to the fat young attendant who had sold them their tickets inside the terminal. As soon as she left the bus, the driver put the bus in gear and pulled slowly out of the station.

They were on their way, but not safely, Susan thought. It was still too easy for Jim to find them. That was why she had to move on to the next part of her plan.

Robbie was looking out the window as they passed a Dairy Queen, a gas station, a bank, and a string of billboards. "Why are we going to St. Louis? Are we going to live there?"

"Would you mind it if we did?"

"It's . . . kinda far away. . . ."

Susan put her arm around Robbie's shoulders. "It is far away . . . for both of us. I know you already miss your friends at school. I'm so sorry, Robbie. I wish we didn't have to do this."

Robbie looked up at Susan and lifted his finger to the bruise on her cheek. "Me, too." Robbie didn't want to tell his mother that he was scared. He could tell she was afraid because she'd started biting her hangnails again, and she always did that when she was scared—like during thunderstorms. Robbie was afraid to leave New Orleans because he'd never known any other home. He would miss the kids at St. Vincent's Sunday School, the kids in his class, and especially his teacher, Mrs. Burris, but not that much. He didn't really have any close, close friends except maybe Jessamyn; she was pretty cool.

Jessamyn was kind of a loner, like he was, and he guessed that was so because she was so smart. Her mother was a professor of metaphysics at LSU; the "other university," his dad would say. Jessamyn was learning to play chess and bridge because her mother wouldn't let her play video games. Jessamyn liked to hang out at Robbie's house because they could play Atari, GameBoy, and Nintendo all they wanted. Yes, Robbie thought, he would miss talking to Jessamyn. Maybe he could sneak away sometime and just call her— sorta let her know he was okay. Yes, he should probably do that, because Jessamyn liked him a lot and she would worry about him.

Robbie was scared to go back to New Orleans, especially now that they had run away. His dad would be really mad now, and Robbie knew he would hurt his mother even more. "I wish I was grown up," Robbie thought to himself. "If I was as old as my dad, I could punch him a couple of times and see how he'd like it. Yes, that's what I would do. I'd take care of Mommy. I wouldn't let him do that again." He glanced up at her, thinking it must be terrible to be a woman, grown up but not strong enough to hit back. At least Robbie was a boy and didn't have to go through life knowing the best he'd ever get out of growing up was to be a woman.

"We're going to start a new life, Robbie. A brand-new life. We're going to meet new people and see new places," Susan said, but Robbie stopped her.

"It's okay, Mommy. I don't want to go back there. It wouldn't be good. It's just that ... I ... I don't know St. Louis. I don't know anyone there. I mean ... Well, how are we going to live? Will you have to go to work every day when I'm at school? Where will we live? What kind of house will we have?"

"House?" Susan was amazed that Robbie was asking

questions faster than she'd been able to formulate her plans. His thinking was more far reaching than hers had been. All this time Susan's thoughts had been focused on "the escape," and she had given only perfunctory analysis to her real future. Susan had been so frightened of Jim, terrified of what he would do to her if he found her, that she'd spent all her time plotting the exactness of her escape route.

Now she realized that Robbie was the one who had zeroed in on the things that should have been her main concerns. She had to find employment. A place to live. God! She'd never lived in anything but a house all her life! She'd never lived on her own. She had gotten pregnant with Robbie at age nineteen and had gone from her parents' lovely home to the three-bedroom brick house Jim had bought the week before the wedding.

She remembered how thrilled she'd been when she saw the small white brick house with green shutters. It was packed neatly only twenty feet from the red brick house next door, as most houses were in landlocked New Orleans, but it was brand-new and smelled of new wood, concrete, and fresh paint. She had loved it at first sight. At the time her parents had grumbled incessantly about the fact that the house was "on the wrong side of Vet's."

"Couldn't you find something on the lake side, dear?"

"It would cost another thirty thousand dollars, Mother, and we can afford this. Once Jim gets his career going, we can move to a larger house," Susan assured her mother.

They never moved. Susan had grown to love the house too much to leave it. Three years ago they had remodeled the house, adding a formal dining room and expanding the living room, adding French doors and a fireplace. Instead of moving to a "better neighborhood," Jim spent his raises on himself.

Susan was happy in her little house with her son . . . for a while.

"I don't think we'll be able to buy a house, Robbie."

"Are we going to live in an apartment like Juan Dominguez?"

"Juan . . . ? Oh, yes. Your friend at Sunday school. Well, I don't know where Juan lives . . . exactly, but I think it might be fun to live in an apartment. They usually have swimming pools and tennis courts we can use."

"They do?"

"Yes."

"Cool, dude," Robbie said cockily and straightened himself up on the high-backed bus seat. His grin filled his face. "This *is* going to be an adventure."

"We'll make it the best adventure yet," Susan assured him.

When the bus stopped in Little Rock Susan and Robbie got off and retrieved their luggage. Susan bought another pair of bus tickets, this time taking them to Houston.

It was midnight when they boarded the night-bound bus to Houston. Robbie was half asleep and totally confused.

"Are you sure we're going in the right direction this time?"

Susan pulled him into her chest so that he could rest his head. "We were always going in the right direction. I just had to do it this way so no one could find us. It's very important that we start our new life totally free of the past. So, that's why I think we should change our names, Robbie."

Robbie scrunched his head around and looked up at her. "I like my name. It's my only name and I'm keeping it."

"Are you adamant about this, or can we discuss it?"

"We can discuss it," he acquiesed just as she knew he would.

"I want us to be free forever, Robbie, and to do that it's almost like we have to become new people. I'm going to change a lot of things about myself. The old Susan was kinda boring, I think. I'm going to cut my hair, maybe change the color. Hmmm. Red, I think."

"Oh, yuck, Mommy."

33

"Okay, brunette."

"Very nice. Are you keeping the same blue eyes?"

She poked his ribs playfully. "Yes, I'm keeping my eyes. But I'm going to put more life in them—more happiness. I want so much more from life than what I've had. I've decided there was a lot about Susan Kidd that was not to be admired. She didn't have much courage, and I'm definitely going to change that."

"I think you have courage."

"I think I do, too. Now, anyway. I've decided that if we're going to live someplace new, they don't have to know what I was like before. Do they?"

"No, I guess not." Robbie considered this line of thinking seriously. He'd never thought people could do that kind of thing—just change everything about themselves like special effects did in movies.

Susan looked out the window at the crystal-clear night as they crossed the border into Texas. "Look at those stars, Robbie. They twinkle and shine perpetually. They never give up. That's it! I'll call myself Star . . . Star Kaiser."

"Oh, that's a wonderful name, Mommy. I like it much better than Susan."

Susan was surprised. "You do?"

"Yes. And now I want a really good name, too. Let's think hard." Robbie had a habit of scrunching his eyebrows together, then placing his thumb under his chin and his forefinger along the top of his chin and looking very stern whenever he was "thinking hard." Susan couldn't help but chuckle when he assumed this facial expression because he actually did look like the CEO of some major corporation in the midst of a mental decision. "I've got it! I want to be called Max!"

"That is a perfect name for you."

"Short for Maxi-million."

"That's Maximilian. He was an emperor, I think."

"I thought it was the name of a rich businessman."

"He was a prince. Just like you."

"Then it's okay, I guess."

"Of course it is. So, we'll be Star and Max Kaiser from . . . where?" She looked quizzically at Robbie, who was very much into the game now.

"New York City; where else?"

"That would work."

"Sure, Mommy. We'd be tough and nobody would mess with us if we were from New York City."

"Not too tough, Max. Don't you pick on other kids or start fights . . ."

"Mommy, don't worry." He suddenly threw his arms around her neck. "I already like these new people we are. I'm gonna like our new life in Houston."

Susan hugged Robbie and kissed the top of his head. She prayed that, even if she was doing the wrong thing with their lives, God would help her put it right.

Chapter Four

Jim Kidd walked out of the most important meeting of his life triumphant. Every man in the firm came up to congratulate him on his success. Men whom Jim had admired for years, men who made in excess of half a million dollars a year in sales, wanted to shake his hand. The president of the firm came down from the ivory tower and walked into the congregation of men in Jim's small but elegant office and placed his own laurels upon Jim.

"Jim, I speak for all the partners when I say that we are very proud of you today. Very proud indeed. It takes a certain kind of energy to begin a business, but it takes persistence and immeasurable determination to keep a company not only rolling, but rocketing into the future. Because of you, we have achieved international status. I couldn't be more grateful."

"Thank you, sir," Jim said humbly. Jim knew that success was sweet, but nothing in his imaginings had prepared him for the incredible rush, the thrill that surged through every cell in his body at that moment.

"Great going, Jim," Henry Kerrigan said and shook Jim's arm until he thought it would fall off.

"You really did it, buddy," Sam Benson said.

"You're the greatest," James Richelieu told him with a wide grin, and then leaned closer to whisper in Jim's ear, "You saved our asses, and don't let anyone tell you otherwise."

Jim's co-workers decided to take Jim out on the town that night to celebrate. They all called their wives and let them know the good news, and that they would be home late. Jim did the same, but there was no answer that afternoon at his house in Metairie. He glanced at his watch and saw that it was three-thirty, a time when Susan normally was home since Robbie would just be getting home from school. "She must have gone to the grocery," he thought to himself. The answering machine clicked on.

"Good news, Susan! Great news! I got the Yamazaki deal. So, the guys are taking me to Bourbon Street to celebrate. Don't wait up. I'll be late."

Jim hung up the phone, never giving Susan a second thought.

In Nacogdoches, Texas, the bus stopped to refuel. Susan ducked into an Eckerd drugstore next to the gas station and bought a pair of scissors, dark brown hair dye, coverup makeup, a pair of cheap bangle earrings in the shape of stars, and a tube of dark red lipstick.

Once the bus drove off, most of the passengers went back to sleep. Robbie had not woken at all when the bus had stopped. Susan utilized this time to go to the bathroom in the bus. Looking into the small mirror, she took stock of her swollen and bruised cheek. The bruise was only beginning to come out, but the tube of coverup would hide the discoloration.

Susan pulled out the scissors. "Good-bye, Susan. Hello,

Star,'' she said, and cut her shoulder-length hair to chin length at the front with a few wispy straight bangs. She gave the back a slight wedge to the best of her ability, thankful the road they were on seemed a smooth one. She would have to get used to cutting her own hair from now on, or at least until she could find a good-paying job. Hair salons were now on the luxury list.

Susan took out the bottle of hair dye and mixed the nearly black dye with the white conditioner in the plastic bottle with the spout. Once it was properly mixed, she placed her hands inside the plastic gloves, took a deep, deep breath, and said good-bye to her naturally sun-streaked blond hair.

In near horror Susan watched as her beautiful golden hair turned brown. In the airplane-sized sink she rinsed the dye out, after waiting the appropriate fifteen minutes, and then used paper towels to blot her head and clean away the dye from her earlobes and neck. She combed the wet dark locks toward her face and was amazed at how much her looks had changed.

Now with the contrast from her dark hair, her blue eyes seemed to jump out of her face. She shaped her lips with the red lipstick and realized she'd never truly appreciated how full and sensuous her mouth was. The dark hair—now a rich, lustrous brown—emphasized her creamy white skin, making her look like a sculpted porcelain doll. She nearly didn't look real. She looked almost too perfect, except for her swollen cheek. She combed her hair over the swelling.

She smiled. ''Perfect.''

Susan gathered up her things and went back to her seat. She felt a newfound sense of security in her disguise and new name. She put Robbie's head on her lap, leaned her head against the window, and shut her eyes. Just as she was about to fall asleep, Robbie opened his sleepy eyes and slowly focused them on his mother.

''Aaaaaaaaaaaah!''

"Shhhhh!"

Susan clamped her hand over Robbie's mouth and quickly scanned the bus to see whether his yelp had awakened anyone, but no one moved. The bus driver gave her a quick scowl in the rearview mirror, but once Robbie quieted down his eyes went back to the dark highway ahead of him.

"Mommy! What happened to you?"

"This is my new disguise."

"When did you buy the wig?"

"It's not a wig. I cut my hair and dyed it."

"Aaaaaaaaaaaah!"

"Robbie . . . shhh!"

"Sorry." He touched her wet hair, then tugged on it. Susan winced. "It's really you."

"You don't like it?"

Robbie grew suddenly serious as he looked her over like a lab technician staring into a microscope. "Hmmm. You look really different. Not prettier, cuz I like the old you, but more like . . . a movie star. You are like Star should be."

"So I fit my name?"

"Sure do."

"And you like it?"

"Yeah. But . . ."

"What, darlin'?"

"Do I have to dye my hair, too?" he asked with near terror in his eyes.

"Oh, no! You don't have to do anything you don't want to do."

"Whew!" he said, theatrically wiping his hand across his forehead. "I like the way I look."

"Me, too."

Robbie laid his head down on her lap and was instantly asleep. Susan looked out the window, but instead of seeing the tall Southern pines along the Texas highway, she saw her reflection in the window. She raised her hand to the glass and touched the downturned corners of the mouth of her image. Shame tinged the edges of her jaw and stole the sparkle from her eyes.

Susan couldn't help thinking about her parents. They had wanted so much for her and her life. They had sheltered her so perfectly inside a cocoon of wealth, social status, and love. She could remember her mother saying, "You're the bubbles in our champagne." The echo of those words had seen her through many a horrid day and night with Jim, when he flung vicious, stinging assaults at her. Later, when the physical abuse began, she forgot the words. She forgot the special person Susan was.

When Susan had become pregnant with Robbie her parents had turned away from her. They had been so ashamed of her, of the "ruin" she'd brought to the family name. Back then she'd wanted to crawl into a hole and die. But she hadn't. She'd forced her parents to accept her again, to love her and Robbie again.

Susan desperately wanted to call her mother and talk to her. She wanted to hear her voice. "Soozahan," her mother would drawl out her name, making it sound more special and dear than it was. Susan had always liked her plain name because of the way her mother would pronounce it. Tears filled Susan's eyes. She couldn't call her mother. She couldn't tell her what she was doing, and she especially couldn't tell her why.

Susan was ashamed of herself for staying with Jim as long as she had. She should have found a way to make him stop drinking. She blamed herself for forcing him to marry her. She should have forced him into therapy. She should have been more understanding. Susan's mind flagellated itself with the should haves, would haves, and could haves. In the end the only thing Susan knew was that she had to get away from Jim and go someplace where he could never find her and hurt her or Robbie again.

The bus pulled to a stop at a country truck stop to refuel. Only three of the passengers disembarked. Susan stared out the window at the pay phones next to the door of the food mart/restaurant. Gently, she lifted Robbie's head from her lap as she scooted out of the seat.

She dug into her jeans pocket for some change. She walked off the bus and went straight to the phone booth.

She placed seven quarters in the slot as directed by the operator and dialed her mother's phone number.

Robbie woke up just then and felt an incredible sense of panic when he realized Susan was missing. "Mommy!"

He bolted to an upright position, realized the bus had stopped, and looked out the window. He saw Susan walking up to the phone booth. He darted out of the seat and dashed down the aisle and out of the bus.

He went racing up to her and put his arms around her waist and pressed his face into her abdomen. "Don't . . ."

The phone was picked up on the other end on the second ring. "Hello?" Annette's groggy, sleep-filled voice answered.

". . . call Daddy . . ." Robbie begged.

Susan's eyes filled with tears. Her hand was shaking as she hung up the receiver and then pulled Robbie into her arms. She sunk her face into his tiny shoulder and let her tears flow. "I wasn't calling Daddy."

"Promise?" Robbie was trembling, his voice choked with emotion and determination.

"Oh, God, Robbie. I hope I'm doing the right thing for us." Susan could barely say the words through her tears. "I love you so much. I don't want you ever, ever, to have a time in your life you can't talk to me. Can't call me." She glanced back to the phone. *Don't be like me. Don't ever be this scared. . . . I'd give anything to know that my parents would love me enough to stand behind me now . . . especially now.* But they clung to old social mores more dearly than they held their daughter. They'd proved that when she'd gotten pregnant. She knew they would surely turn on her now for running away. As Susan, she was just another wife, another mother stuck in the mire of the bad decisions she'd made for herself. A tear trickled down her cheek. She needed to talk to them, but they didn't need or want to hear about her problems. Sadly, her parents were ill-equipped to deal with hard-life problems. Their lives had been insulated from pain and loss through blessed luck. There was nothing in Bart's or Annette's backgrounds that would have prepared them for this situation. How could they possibly understand something like wife abuse or the real threat of child abuse?

Susan hugged Robbie tighter. "Promise me, okay?"

"I . . . I promise . . . Mommy." Robbie was sobbing as he wrapped his arms and legs around her like a monkey as she carried him back to the bus.

Susan held Robbie when the bus drove away from the truck stop. Robbie laid his head on Susan's lap and was instantly asleep.

Susan looked at her reflection in the window. She looked so very different, stronger and not so vulnerable. "Star . . . I hope you learn how to shine."

Jim nearly reeled out of Brennan's, still riding high on exhilaration. Sure, he'd had a few drinks—four, maybe five—but who was counting? He was out with the guys, and they never nagged him like Susan *always* did. They were cool. They didn't pressure him at all.

"Wher'we goin' now?" Jim asked with a slight slur to his words.

"I gotta check out," James said. "I've got an early morning and Janice is waiting for me."

"Yeah, me, too," Henry said. "My kids have barely seen me since this whole Japanese campaign started. Man, I'm beat."

Jim turned to Sam. "Whatdya say, Sam? Let's go over to

Pat O'Brien's and see what we can scare up.''

"I can't, Jim. I've got to finish my reports tomorrow, and then fly up to Chicago to meet with Banker's Trust. I really shouldn't have taken this much time away from work.''

Jim slapped Sam on the back. "Aw, c'mon. You're not gonna make me celebrate alone, are ya?''

Sam was firm when he took Jim's hand off his shoulder. "Look, pal, it's after eleven. It'll be midnight before I make it across the bridge to my house. Besides, I think you've done enough celebrating for all of us.''

"Bullshit.'' Jim slipped his hand into his pants pocket and missed. He stumbled.

"Let me drive you home. You've had too many.''

"Th' fu . . . I have.''

Sam was becoming perturbed. "I'm driving you home, Jim. The Benz is perfectly safe in the Royal Sonesta parking lot. I'll come by in the morning, pick you up, and we'll get your car then.'' He looked to the others for support.

James was first to react. "Sam's right. C'mon, Jim. Let's go home.''

"Awright, awright. You guys aren't any fun, anyway.'' Jim laughed and they all laughed with him.

At dawn Susan and Robbie walked off the bus at the Houston downtown bus terminal, lugging their suitcases along. "Stay close, Robbie,'' Susan said as she glanced from side to side, seeing people who looked as if they hadn't bathed in a month, or had a change of clothes in a year, sleeping in the chairs and along the benches in the terminal. They frightened her, these people who looked forgotten, but they were oblivious to her. They had problems of their own, she thought.

"Max, Mom. You gotta call me Max.''

"Yeah, right.'' She stopped dead still. "Since when did you start calling me 'Mom'?''

Robbie rolled his eyes. "Since I became Max.''

43

"Oh," she said and smiled.

Max grinned back at her.

Susan went outside the terminal, where a row of vending machines held the local newspapers, *USA Today*, and the *Wall Street Journal*. Susan inserted two quarters and bought a *Houston Chronicle*. They huddled against the building, making certain their bags and luggage were propped against the wall, and used their bodies as protection against the stares they were starting to receive.

While Susan combed the apartment section, Robbie watched the people on the street. They looked at him as if he were from outer space. Was it possible they knew he was here under an assumed name? Naw. He was afraid, and because he was scared of this new place and these strange people, his eyes were playing tricks on him. These people weren't really staring at him any more than normal. He took a deep breath and told himself to relax.

Robbie looked across the street to a row of garbage cans surrounded by black trash bags filled with garbage. Suddenly one of the bags rolled and then moved. Robbie realized that a homeless person had used the bag to protect himself from the rainfall earlier that night. Next to the man in the garbage bag was a woman who sat with her back against a concrete building and had surrounded herself with her belongings, making what looked like walls around her. As he watched her arranging and then rearranging her bags and sacks, he realized she was creating a home.

Robbie looked down at the way he was guarding his possessions and then back at the woman who used her belongings as if they could protect her from the hopelessness around her.

Robbie hoped he would never be truly homeless, the way these people were.

"God, I can't believe this . . . Max." Susan remembered to call him by his new name. "The places that have the lowest rents . . . ones we can afford, don't allow children."

"Mom, I'm a child. We can't change that." He grabbed part of the paper and looked at the photograph ads. "Some of these look awesome."

"And more expensive than I thought." Susan realized that in order to save money she would have to move farther out of the city—way out. "Here, on the north side, are some apartments we could afford, and they allow children."

"All right, Star!" Robbie gave Susan a high five.

Susan and Robbie went back inside the terminal to a phone booth, where she called the apartment complex. She was told there was a vacancy and to bring her driver's license and two paycheck stubs to prove her employment.

Susan then went to the ticket window and inquired about the city bus system. She was directed to the proper bus stop and informed where to transfer buses and how much it would cost.

As they rode the nearly hour-long commute to North Houston, Robbie read the ad about the complex that would be their new home. "It says here we can have pets. Max needs a puppy, Mom."

Susan couldn't help smiling to herself. Jim had never allowed any pets in the house, or the yard, for that matter. Jim's argument that a dog would "tear up the yard" had made sense at the time, when Susan was planting and landscaping and forcing seedlings to grow in the poor New Orleans soil. As a baby, Robbie was always so sick with ear infections that the care of a dog or cat would have been just another thing for Susan to be responsible for. Robbie was older now, and with no brothers or sisters a pet might not be such a bad idea.

"Who's going to feed the puppy?"

"I will."

"And paper train it, housebreak it, shampoo it, brush it, walk it, scoop its poop?"

"Boy! Is a puppy that much trouble? I was just going to love it."

Susan laughed. "You can have a puppy."

Robbie was shocked at Susan's quick response. "Maybe we should think about it."

The bus took the Kuykendahl exit off I-45 and traveled north. Just past FM 1960 the bus stopped and Susan and Robbie got off. The driver had told Susan that the apartment complex she was looking for was only a short distance away, but when she inquired as to the exact address at the Texaco station on the corner, the mechanic, who looked to be about nineteen, took one look at all their luggage and laughed.

"Where you all from, darlin'? New York?"

Susan looked at Robbie. She'd forgotten the plan.

Robbie spoke up immediately. "Yes. How did you know?"

"See it all the time down here. New Yorkers . . . takes 'em a little longer to catch on."

"Catch on to what?" Susan asked.

"Well, that apartment complex is about four miles up the road here." He pointed north. "This is Texas . . . it's a big place. We're kinda sprawled out. We like lots of elbow room. So, when a feller says to you that somethin' is 'jes' down the road a piece' you can usually figger it's about five miles."

"Ah." Susan nodded her head. She was already hot standing in the sun. It was going to be a long walk. "Is there another bus?"

"Not the way you're goin'. Sorry. It'd take forever to get a cab. Mighty expensive, too."

"I guess we'll have to walk."

The mechanic pulled an oily blue cloth from his back pocket and wiped his greasy hands. Susan wasn't so sure that he didn't put more grease on his hands than was already present. "If you wait just a few minutes till my break, I'll drive you up there."

"Why, that's very kind of you, but I—"

Robbie cut in immediately. "Thanks a lot." Robbie nodded his head assertively and stuck out his hand. "My name's Max. This is my mom. You can call her Star."

The mechanic smiled sheepishly. "A real purty name for a purty lady."

"Why, thank you . . ."

"Mike."

"Thank you, Mike."

"Yer welcome."

Mike left and went back to the car he was repairing. Susan and Robbie walked around to the back of the sparkling-clean station, which was more beautifully landscaped than Susan's backyard in New Orleans, and sat on a curb beneath a cluster of tall Southern pines. A breeze wafted through the air, swirling a warm, musky pine fragrance with it. Susan inhaled deeply of the clean air. Houston was better than New Orleans; she knew it from this very moment. It was open and big and free, just as Mike had said. Everyone had space here. They weren't crammed next to each other the way they were in New Orleans, everyone fighting for their tiny patch of ground; a physical reality that Susan always believed had to leave some sort of impression on the soul. There was no stench here from open canals, and the air moved through the trees rather than hanging from the branches like old laundry. There was an excitement here, a sense of adventure she'd never felt in New Orleans. It was odd, but Susan felt as if she'd finally come home.

True to his word, Mike drove "Star" and "Max" to the apartment complex and wouldn't take any money for his effort.

"Glad t' hep out," he said with a wide, friendly grin and waved to her as he drove back to the gas station.

Robbie turned to his mother. "You go talk to them, Mom. I'll guard our stuff," he said, sitting down atop the suitcases and holding the WalMart bag close to his chest.

"Okay," she said and walked inside.

The woman sitting at the desk was about thirty-five years old with streaked blond hair, a suntanned body, and minimal makeup. The minute Susan walked in, she smiled brightly and rose.

"Hello!" she said, extending her hand. "You must be the woman who called earlier. Mrs. Kaiser, isn't it? M'name's Andrea, but you can call me Andie. Everybody does."

"Nice to meet you, Andie. I'm Star Kaiser." Susan wondered how long it would take to say her name without thinking about it. "You have a one-bedroom for rent?"

"I certainly do. It was vacated yesterday. I've got the key right here, so I can show it to you."

Susan put up her hand. "I'd like to get the paperwork over with first."

"But, honey, you need to see if the apartment is suitable to you. I always say, there's nothin' worse than bein' a horse in the wrong corral."

Susan knew that her eyes kept glancing out the window at Robbie, sitting atop their belongings. Suddenly she realized how odd this might look to Andie. She had no furniture, no appliances to move in. There was only her and Robbie. "I'm sure it's perfect."

Andie followed Susan's eyes to the window. The second she saw Robbie, she knew exactly Susan's situation. Andie came from around the desk and looked at Susan quite pointedly.

"Do you have the papers I told you to bring?"

"I . . . uh . . . ."

"I need your Social Security Number, driver's license, two paycheck stubs or a letter from an employer. I need first and last month's rent and a security deposit of two hundred dollars. You can write a check, of course."

Susan nearly dropped her jaw, but it still hurt too much. What in God's name had she been thinking all this time? She'd never rented anything in her life, and she had no idea it was nearly as difficult as buying a house. Maybe more so. What was she going to do? She had to think quick.

"My Social Security Number is 314–70–8900. I just moved here from New York City and I never drove in the city, I took cabs, so I have no license. I don't have a job here, but I intend to get one after *you* tell me where I can find something so that I can support myself and my son. I'm not choosy; waiting tables is not beneath me. I had plenty of experience in New York, since I had to wait tables while I was trying to get an acting job on a soap opera . . ."

Andie was unmoved during Susan's monologue until she said the words *soap opera*. "Goddammit, honey! I *knew* I recognized you! You're that girl on 'The Bold and the Beautiful,' or was it 'Santa Barbara'? Did that go off the air? I don't watch them myself, mind you, since I have to keep a close watch on the office here, but I do pick up that *Soap Opera Digest* every so often."

"I'm not really . . ."

"Aw, c'mon, you can tell me. I won't snitch." Andie took a closer look at Susan and saw the bruise under her makeup. "Gee whilikers, honey. Did some actor boyfriend do that to you?" Andie slid her arm around Susan's waist. "Don't you worry about a thing. This will be our little secret. I understand everything now. I'll help you all I can."

Andie sat Susan down in the stained wing chair opposite her desk. She moved the copper pot filled with plastic flowers to the side and sat on the desk. "What else do you need besides the apartment?"

"A job."

"Not much call for actresses around here."

Susan knew that arguing the point with this woman was useless. She was going to believe what she wanted to believe. "I'll take anything . . . for now."

"Do you have a degree?"

"No." Susan instantly felt that old sting of shame for not

getting her college education. She wished she *had* listened to her parents about that . . . sometimes.

"Graduate high school?"

"Yes."

"That's good. What experience do you have? Secretarial? Clerical? You do know how to run a computer, don't you?"

"No . . . none of that."

"Gees, honey. I guess you'll have to wait tables for a while, but that's okay. It's honest work, right?"

"Is there anyplace around here?"

"Sure. In fact, the Chili's just up the street might need some help. We'll call them later."

"Exactly how far away are they?"

Andie walked around to the back of her desk and pulled out the drawer that held the applications-for-rent forms. "Oh, six, seven miles."

Susan nodded. "Just down the road a piece."

Andie smiled. "That's right." She handed Susan the forms. "Fill these out. How are you going to pay for the rent? MasterCard?"

Susan's eyes flew open. "I could put my rent on a charge card?"

"Sure can." Andie smiled broadly.

"Amazing." Susan took the ballpoint pen Andie offered her. "Here's my deal. I give you fifteen hundred in cash for six-months' rent in advance. No security deposit. I have a neatnik for a child."

"It's a deal. And I promise I won't tell anyone about your real identity. For their information, you are Mrs. Star Kaiser."

"That's my name," Susan said proudly, knowing that, in a million years, Susan Kidd would never have had the courage, the daring, to make a deal like the one she'd just made. Susan was beginning to wonder if she shouldn't have been named Star from birth. It fit her so well.

Chapter Five

Jim Kidd managed to insert his house key into the lock on the fourth try. He turned around and waved to Sam, who was waiting in his car to see that Jim got in the house under his own power. Sam hit the high beam on his headlights and backed out of the drive.

"Jerk," Jim mumbled as Sam drove away. Jim detested being treated like an invalid just because he'd had a couple of drinks. Good thing he didn't tell the guys he'd been drinking doubles, or they would have razzed him even more.

Jim threw his briefcase to the floor and it landed with a hard, slapping sound. Goddammit. What was wrong with everybody lately that they all thought he was some kind of incompetent because he'd had a few lousy drinks? Why couldn't things be the way they used to be? Susan gave him hell; but then, she'd been giving him hell for five years. Even Susan's father, Bart, had told him at the last family dinner that he'd had too much to drink and Susan should drive the car home. At the time Jim hadn't cared. She could drive. He was tired anyway.

But now even the guys were giving him grief. Goddammit. He had pressures. So what if he had a drink now and then? So what? He wasn't hurting anybody. Jim turned on the light in the living room. He looked straight ahead into the family room and the eat-in kitchen.

Suddenly he felt as if he were suspended in time, and then he was catapulted back to the night before. Was he having déjà vu? He had walked into the house just as he had tonight, but Susan had been there, greeting him with a smile. Then all of a sudden she'd started saying he was drunk. She'd told him to leave. Leave his own damn house! Was she crazy?

That must be it: Susan was crazy. He'd heard that it happened sometimes to housewives who stayed home with their children all the time. They lost their brain cells and went crazy. Jim was certain he'd read about that in the *Wall Street Journal.* He remembered making precisely that point to Susan last night.

"You're crazy, Susan. Loco. Nuts. I think you should see a psychiatrist."
"Me?"
"Yes, you."
"You're an alcoholic, Jim. You're sick and you need medical attention. It's a disease—"
"Shut the hell up!" he'd screamed, and hit her.

He'd hit her. Jim had hit Susan.

Jim watched the scene roll before his eyes as if he were inside that space and time all over again. He was shocked at what he saw. He hadn't done that! He hadn't hit his wife!

"Oh God." Jim staggered suddenly and backed into the sofa. He plopped down, still stunned at what he'd done. "I couldn't have." He dropped his face into his hands. His splayed hands slowly dragged down his cheeks and he knew the truth. "I hit her. Again."

He shook his head, hoping to unhinge the last of the cob-webs in his brain. "I promised I would never do that again. . . ."

Jim looked around him now, suddenly sober. He noticed that the house was perfectly spotless, as always. Robbie's toys were put away, as always. But something was wrong. It was quiet, yes, as it should be at twelve forty-five at night, but this was something different. Something didn't feel right. The house didn't feel right to him.

He stood instantly. "Susan?" Her name was barely a whis-per.

Panic hit him like an atomic bomb. "Susan!" He raced through the living room, down the hall to the bedrooms, past Robbie's room, directly to his room . . . his and Susan's room.

Moonlight flooded the room through the lace curtains, etch-ing a flower pattern on the bed and furnishings. In the dark-ness he couldn't see a lump in the bed where Susan's body should be. Jim's hand was shaking when he hit the light switch. *"Susan!"*

He went to the bed and felt it. She was here. He knew she was here. She *had* to be here. It was his eyes; his eyes were playing tricks on him. It was the booze. It had made him temporarily blind. That was all.

Jim felt every inch of the bed, crawled on top of it and patted and clutched at the coverlet like a madman. Tears came to his eyes, cleansing away the alcoholic fog. "Susan. Susan. Uuuuuuugh," he screamed at the silent, empty room. His stomach knotted, then seemed to fall out of his body. "Susan . . . Don't leave me."

"If you ever come near me again, I'll leave you, Jim," she had said last January, when he'd hit her for the first time. For two weeks he couldn't look at her. He didn't sleep with her, eat with her, talk to her, because to do so was to look at himself. Jim Kidd felt he could do nearly anything in this world except look at himself.

He was fine, he told himself, as he tried to calm down. He felt as if he'd just fallen from a ten-story building. He didn't want to feel this way . . . and why should he, anyway? He'd always been fine. Susan was the one who was high-strung. Yes, that was it. She'd overreacted to the situation. So, maybe he could cut back on the drinking a bit. No big deal. He could do that. It was the pressures at work. This Japanese deal had nearly driven them all insane. Even James said he couldn't wait to have a normal life again. This was just a simple little mistake.

Jim pushed his face into the pillow . . . Susan's pillow. It still smelled of Opium perfume. "Susan . . ." His fingers curled around the coverlet and he yanked on the fabric as hard as he could.

Dammit, he thought angrily. She couldn't do this to him. She couldn't make him feel this way, as if he'd just lost everything in the world. She was his wife, goddammit. She was his. She couldn't just leave, walk out just because things got a bit tough. That's what life was all about, wasn't it? Through the hard times and the good.

Now he knew what kind of person Susan was. Oh, she stuck around for the good times, but when things didn't go just her way she checked out. Jim balled his fist and hit the bed. "Bitch. Lousy, selfish bitch!"

He rammed his fist into the bed again. He pretended it was Susan. "Bitch!" Suddenly he stopped in mid-motion. What was he doing? He didn't really want to hit Susan. But goddammit, he was mad. Real mad.

Jim bolted off the bed and looked around the room. All Susan's things were just where she'd left them. Her sterling silver–framed photographs still lined the deep windowsill in the bay window. He went to the bureau and pulled out the drawers. Everything looked in order. But, no. No. Her nightgown was gone. He dashed to the closet and ran his hand down the rail on her side. Nothing was missing. Her shoes

54

were perfectly arranged on the shoe rack, just like always. He went to the bathroom and found that all her makeup was undisturbed. His eyes searched the room again. The top of the bureau was still adorned with her perfume bottles. As his eyes focused on the cluster of designer perfumes, his mind started clicking.

He turned on the crystal bedside lamp. He walked to the bureau and tickued off the list of perfumes: "Passion, Obsession, Hererra, Opium . . . bingo!" Jim smiled to himself.

"Susan wouldn't go overnight to her mother's without her Opium." This was a sure sign that even though Susan was gone tonight, she didn't intend to stay away for long. Susan was just trying to teach him a lesson. Well, he'd teach her a thing or two, he thought.

Jim went back to the bed. Sitting down next to the telephone, he picked up the receiver. He dialed the lakeside home of Bart and Annette Beaulieu, his in-laws.

"Sorry to wake you, Annette, but could I please speak to Susan?"

Annette cleared her throat of sleep. "Susan? What are you talking about, Jim?"

"I want to speak with my wife, if you don't mind."

"Jim, is this some kind of joke?"

"I hardly think so."

There was a long pause on the other end of the line. Annette's voice moved an octave higher as fear rattled through her mind. "Are you saying that my daughter is not home . . . at twelve forty-nine in the morning?"

Jim decided not to play into Annette's obviously well-rehearsed responses. "Are you going to put Susan on the phone or not?"

"Where's Robbie, Jim?" Annette asked.

"Robbie?"

"Your son. I'll bet you haven't even thought to look in his room."

"Hell." Jim threw down the phone and raced out of the bedroom. He turned on the light in Robbie's room. His bed was unmade, but Robbie wasn't in it. He banged his fist against the wall and then raced back to the phone.

"Put her on," he demanded.

"I can't put her on the phone, Jim, because she's not here. What I want to know is *why* she isn't with you. Did you two have another fight?"

"What do you mean 'another fight'? Susan and I have never exchanged words."

"The way I hear it, you use your fists to handle your problems."

Jim knew for a fact that Susan would never tell her parents anything disparaging about their life together. Ever since Susan got pregnant, she had purposefully kept herself distant from her parents, a practice Jim supported—to a degree. Jim needed Bart and Annette as much as—no, more, than he needed Susan. Bart had gotten him his job at Metro Media, and Bart's very substantial influence on the New Orleans business community was worth all the sucking up Jim had done over the years.

Jim decided to call Annette's bluff. "Did Susan ever tell you that I hurt her?"

"No. She hasn't."

"Has she ever insinuated that our marriage was anything short of blissful?"

"No."

"Then how can you say such a thing to me, Annette? We're family."

Jim thought he could hear the ladylike growl Annette used whenever she became angry. "I heard it from Rabina Parker. She saw Susan one day last winter when she'd dropped off the AIDS Charity Ball tickets."

"Rabina Parker has been jealous of Susan for years and

you know it. She'd say anything to make you think ill of me or Susan."

"So you say. But it still doesn't discard the fact that your wife is not at home with you now. Did you just get home yourself, Jim?"

"Yes, I did, as a matter of fact. I closed the Yamazaki deal today, and all of us from the office went to Brennan's for dinner tonight."

"Late supper."

"Annette . . . are we through with the twenty-questions routine? Where is Susan?"

"I don't know, Jim. She's not here. I haven't heard from her for about three days now, which isn't unusual because I've been so busy with the annual fundraiser for the Oshner Clinic children's ward."

"Damn."

"Jim, I'm worried. Susan wouldn't really leave you, would she?"

"Oh, no. In fact, I've checked, and nothing seems to be missing except that old ugly cotton nightgown she loves."

"You didn't fight, then?"

"It's nothing serious, Annette. I've been overworked and she's been complaining about the fact that I should help out around the house more. She's probably at Cynthia's down the street. She wanted to teach me a lesson and she sure did. I'll have to buy her some roses and take her out to dinner to make it up to her. Now that my deal is closed I can help her out. It's tough taking care of the house and Robbie by herself, I know."

"Jim, do me a favor: Don't lie to me. You're not the house-husband type. Hire her a maid like you should have done years ago and be done with it. Then I won't have to get any more of these midnight calls. Tell Susan to call me in the morning and I'll take her to lunch."

"All right. Thanks, Annette."

"Good night, Jim." Annette hung up.

Jim nearly leapt off the bed. "Son-of-a-bitch! She wouldn't go to Cynthia's if it was the last place on earth."

Jim began pacing. *Think, man. Did you hit her hard? Does it show? Where can she go where no one will ask her questions?* Jim's mind whirled with the possibilities. Suddenly he snapped his fingers as it hit him. He raced to the kitchen, grabbed the Yellow Pages, and picked up the telephone. If it took him all night long, he would call every hotel in New Orleans until he found his wife and brought her home.

Jim was exhausted by the time he'd made his way through the New Orleans Yellow Pages. He called every motel and hotel in the city, in Metairie, Kenner, across the river in Gretna, and even as far out as Slidell. There was no sign of Susan or Robbie anywhere.

As Jim started to fall asleep, fully dressed, on the bed, he was convinced that Susan would come back home today after she'd had a chance to cool off and rethink her options should she truly leave him.

His ace in the hole was that Susan had never lived anyplace but New Orleans all her life. Her insular world had not equipped her for life anywhere else but here. Susan was a creature of habit. Change of any kind made her nuts. That was probably why she'd been unable to handle the stress they'd all been under lately because of the Japanese deal.

Yes, Jim thought to himself as sleep overtook him, Susan would come home. She had no place else to go.

Chapter Six

"It's kinda small, isn't it?" Robbie said to Susan when they walked into their new apartment. The living room/dining room was a perfect uninteresting square, newly carpeted in cheap, wheat-colored carpet. A small galley kitchen sat off to the left and the bedroom and bath were off to the right. It had been freshly painted, but the light fixtures were out of date and cast meager light. The kitchen was equipped with a dishwasher, garbage disposal, refrigerator, and stove.

Robbie flung down his WalMart bag and began investigating. He rattled off the inadequacies he found. "No ice maker. No water through the door. No microwave. No under-the-counter can opener. No sprayer in the sink. The faucet leaks." He opened the dishwasher door with difficulty. "The door must be broken."

"It just needs to be greased."

"Oh." He raced to the bathroom. "No shower curtain?" He came walking back out with his hands on his hips. "How am I supposed to take a shower without a shower curtain?"

59

"I guess we'll have to buy one." Susan looked around the apartment and made her own mental notes. At least a hundred dollars for some kind of curtains on the windows. Twenty bucks for the cheap dishes she'd seen at WalMart. Silverware, pots, pans, dishrags, towels, linens. Beds. God in heaven! They didn't have a bed to sleep in. Pillows, blankets. Food. Spices, sugar, flour, staples, cleaning tools, broom, mop, cleansers were all necessary. She didn't need Robbie's calculator to know that without the first stick of furniture and certainly not the luxury of a bed, her list would cost over five hundred dollars.

Susan felt sick to her stomach. She had a roof over her head, but that was all. And that only lasted for six months. Her cashier's check for three thousand dollars wouldn't last long, but at least she had it.

"What are we gonna do about furniture?" Robbie asked Susan.

"We'll check the newspaper for used pieces. Until I get a job we'll have to be really careful."

"I understand." Robbie went to his WalMart bag and retrieved the newspaper they'd bought earlier that morning. He laid out the paper on the floor in the middle of the living room and stretched out on his stomach. He propped up his elbows and placed his face in his hands. "What do I look under?"

"Used furniture," Susan called from the bedroom, where she'd gone with the garment bag. She unzipped it and took out her dresses and hung them on the pole in the narrow closet. She placed her boxes of shoes on the floor. She stood there staring at the empty floor.

If she'd been catapulted to another planet, Susan couldn't have felt any more out of touch with her surroundings. What was she doing here? Was this all worth it? How could she ask Robbie to give up his life when it was *her* life that needed changing? Her hand flew to her throat as she felt icy fingers of fear begin to choke her.

"Don't listen to the demons," Susan said aloud. "Don't listen to them." Susan remembered the old saying she'd learned from the second-grade nun in Catholic school. So many times that little phrase had helped her when she'd been afraid.

She quickly shut the closet door and realized there was a full-length mirror on the other side. She stared at her reflection. She touched her cheek. *He could have broken it. Maybe next time he would have. Maybe next time he wouldn't have stopped. What if the next time became another next time until you were dead, Susan? Then what would Robbie do?*

She placed her hands on the mirror and lowered her forehead to the glass. *You did the right thing. You did the right thing.*

"Queen size or king, Mom?" Robbie yelled from the other room.

"Double if you can find it." She looked up. "The sheets cost less," she whispered aloud.

New Orleans

When Jim walked into the office that day, the secretaries had pooled their money and bought him a horseshoe of flowers and had it propped against his desk. Three mylar balloons emblazoned with the words "Congratulations" were tied to the back of his desk chair. The telephone was ringing. Jim raced to answer it, hoping it was Susan.

"She'd better have a good explanation for putting me through all this," he said to himself as he lifted the receiver.

"Jim Kidd, here."

"Mr. Yamoto on line three, sir."

"Thanks, Beverly."

Jim took the call from his newest and most important client. Even though Mr. Yamoto told Jim that his board had voted in favor of giving Metro Media their new porcelain company's advertising as well as their two main divisions, Jim's reaction was deflated. Jim was gracious and assured Mr. Yamoto that he would give all their divisions his undivided attention. When Jim hung up the phone he wondered why he was unmoved by this third coup.

It's Susan's fault. If she'd been home where she was supposed to be, I wouldn't be in such a bad mood.

Just then the phone rang, and Jim's secretary announced the arrival of his appointment. Jim thanked her for the flowers and made a mental note to do something nice for the girls in the office. Then he gathered up his reports and left his office for the conference room, where he would make advertising history again.

Houston, Texas

When Susan heard the knock on her apartment door she nearly leapt off the floor. Robbie ran to her and hugged her, his eyes wide with fright.

"No one knows we're here," Robbie said.

"Who . . . who is it?" Susan called to the closed door.

"Andie."

Susan and Robbie both expelled a huge sigh of relief. "Coming," Susan said and opened the door.

Andie was all smiles. And parcels. Andie was loaded down with boxes of cleaning supplies, paper towels, a bag of ice, a six pack of Cokes, and a box of cookies.

"What is all this?" Susan asked.

"I know it's gonna be a while till your furniture arrives from New York." Andie winked conspiratorily at Robbie.

He winked back at her, looked at Susan, and shrugged his shoulders.

"I knew you could use a few things. So, I brought some

snacks for your son. I know I always like to clean things myself before I use them . . . especially the bathroom . . . I thought you might be the same.''

''Oh, yes, thank you. I'm so—''

''Don't go on, honey. We've all had times like this when we're just kinda at sixes and sevens. I just wanted to tell you that down in storage are some things—furniture and such— that tenants have left here over the years, and rather than throw them out I've always kept them . . . for emergencies. If you know what I mean.'' She winked at Robbie again.

Again he winked back.

''Here's the key to the storage room. Go around the pool, and behind the mailboxes in the rear of the complex is a beige-sided building with tan trim. No windows. That's the storage. Just help yourself. If you need some of the bigger pieces, I'll get one of the fellas around here to move them for you.''

''I . . . I can't believe this! Are you an angel or something?'' Susan wanted to hug the woman but felt that Andie would think her too effusive.

Andie patted Susan on the back. ''Lots of us have been there, honey. You just take care of that sweet little boy, okay? And I'll talk to you later.'' Andie whooshed out the door.

Robbie's jaw was slack as he stared at the closed door. ''That is one silly lady, but she sure is nice. Huh, Mom?''

''Yes. She is very nice.'' Susan looked down at the key.

Robbie didn't waste a second. He grabbed Susan's hand. ''C'mon, Mom. Let's go see what she's got!''

''Okay!''

They raced out of the apartment, practically skipping down the winding sidewalk, through the pines and begonia beds strewn with pine nettles, around the pool to the mailboxes and dumpster and to the storage house.

Susan unlocked the door and opened it.

''Wheeeeweeee! What stinks?'' Robbie asked as he waved

his hand across his face and pinched his nose with his thumb and forefinger.

"Mildew. This room isn't air-conditioned."

"Hey! Look! A cowboy lamp!" Robbie picked up a very old wooden lamp. Someone had burned cattle brands into the base and the shade. "This is neat. Can I have it?"

"I don't see why not."

Susan dug past a stack of wooden boxes and found a coffee table that someone's dog had cut teeth on. "We could sand this down and it would be just fine. It's rather rustic and goes with your lamp, Robbie."

In the far corner was an old leather easy chair with a great deal of brass upholstery tacks for trim. "I bet if we got some saddle soap this chair might not be bad either."

Robbie found an end table that matched the coffee table and a sleeping bag, which he held up for his mother to see. "Think we could wash this?"

Susan turned her head away. "I'm afraid not. It smells like someone let their horse sleep in it."

"Yeah," Robbie agreed and flung it aside quickly as if it were infested with lice.

Susan found a box filled with gas-station giveaway glasses, and in another box she discovered chipped plates, mugs, and even a frying pan.

"I never thought I would be so happy to see someone else's junk."

Robbie looked at his mother. "All those times we gave our old stuff to the church . . . I guess it really did help somebody, huh?"

"Yes. I'm sure of it now." She tousled his hair and smiled. "Well, let's see how much of this we can get up to our place, and then we'll ask Andie if we can use her telephone to call about that bed you found."

"Great!" Robbie said, grasping his lamp in one hand and a small cigar box in the other.

"What's in there?"

"Somebody's Matchbox cars," he said proudly. "I think I might need 'em."

"I'm sure you do," she said as she held the door for him.

That night, with Andie's help and a pickup truck borrowed from Luis Perrera, one of the tenants in the complex, Susan, Robbie, Luis, and Luis's girlfriend, Micaela, bought a queen-sized bed from a woman in Terra Nova for seventy-five dollars.

Susan and Robbie agreed to ride in the back of the truck and hold the mattress down for safekeeping. It was a beautiful clear night and the air was filled with the scent of pine. Again Susan's spirits were lifted, knowing that she had new friends and that, though her new home was very different than her old one, she could be happy here.

New Orleans

At the same time that Susan was setting up her new bed in Houston Jim was pacing the floor in his living room, the telephone receiver in one hand and a list of emergency numbers in the other.

"I want to report a missing person—two missing persons. My wife and my son."

"When did you discover their disappearance?"

"They're gone, okay?" Jim knew he was short with the man, but he didn't care. He was generally pissed about the whole matter.

"Sir, we cannot report anyone missing until twenty-four hours has passed."

"Oh. I didn't know that. I'm sorry. It's just that—"

"I know, sir. This is a very difficult and frightening time for anyone."

"Yes. Difficult. Day before yesterday," Jim replied, hoping the police wouldn't pin him down any more than that, because the truth was, he didn't know when Susan had left. Did she leave at night after he'd hit her? Did she stay till morning? Had she even left and come back during the day and he hadn't known about it? His mind was a mass of confusion. He needed a drink. He licked his lips and tried to focus on the questions he was being asked.

"Are there any signs they were forcibly taken from your home?"

"Of course not, but . . . Officer, that had never entered my mind. How would I know if they'd been taken?" Jim's eyes scanned the house.

"A door broken down, a lock broken, a broken window . . ."

"No. No. Susan was the worst, the worst about keeping the house locked while I was at work. She was always in and out of the garden and the French doors were hardly ever locked. Could someone jump the fence?"

"It's possible. Is anything missing from the house?"

"Hardly anything of Susan's; a nightgown, that's all. I did notice that Robbie's calculator is gone."

"Nothing else of your son's things is missing?"

"I can't tell . . . No. Nothing."

"Your wife—if she was abducted at night, would she have been wearing the nightgown you spoke of?"

"Yes. It was her favorite."

"Sir, before you get upset, there is another question I have to ask you."

"Shoot."

"Did you and your wife have any arguments recently?"

"Not really."

"Nothing. You get along well with your wife?"

"Of course." Jim ran his shaking hand across his forehead.

He looked at his hand. He hoped he never had to take a lie detector test; he'd be spotted in a flash. "My wife is a very contented woman. However, I may have had a bit too much to drink that night, and I suppose she might have taken a few things I said the wrong way. You know how women are."

"Yes, sir. I do." The officer paused for a moment. "Mr. Kidd, you'll have to come down to headquarters and file a report. Ask for me—Sergeant Brian Patterson."

"Fine. I'll be right there. . . . Oh, and Sergeant Patterson, you think my wife was kidnapped?"

"No, sir. I think your wife ran away."

Jim was stunned. He suddenly couldn't think. "Th—thank you, Sergeant Patterson. I'll see you in few minutes."

"Take your time, Mr. Kidd." Sergeant Patterson hung up.

Jim picked up his double-breasted, Italian-cut suit coat and slipped his arms into the silk-lined sleeves. He buttoned the bottom button and ran his hands over the expensive cloth, making certain it hung perfectly.

Susan . . . ran . . . away. . . . His mind focused on each word so that he could grasp their elusive meaning. None of these words could fit in the same sentence together, Jim thought to himself. Susan couldn't, would never leave him. Not really. She'd threatened him with many things over the past few years, when she was nagging him about his drinking or not doing some chores or not spending time with Robbie. But all wives did that, didn't they?

What had happened to Susan that she would become so mentally unbalanced all of a sudden and leave him?

If she wanted a divorce, why didn't she file for one like a normal woman and demand half the furniture, the car, and visitation rights?

Jim picked up his keys from the mahogany secretary. As he turned toward the door, he remembered an argument he'd had with Susan, standing in this very spot over four years earlier.

"I'm not going with you, Jim. You're drunk. You're a danger to yourself, me, and everyone else on the road when you're in this condition."

"I am not drunk. I've driven home like this hundreds of times. Now come on. We're going!" He'd grabbed her arm and yanked on it.

She twisted away from him. "No!"

"Fine. I'll go by myself." He started toward the door.

"You walk out that door, Jim Kidd, and I'll file for divorce in the morning."

Rage blasted through Jim like a Gulf Coast hurricane. "You'll what?"

"File . . . for divorce." She stood firmly on both feet, with too much determination in her eyes.

"You do and I'll fight you in every court in this country for custody of Robbie. It'll be the last goddamn time you ever see that kid of yours."

"Why would you do that? You barely notice his existence now."

"To keep you from him. He's my son."

"But he's not your property."

Jim ground his jaw angrily. "How far do you think you'd get in this state when you have no source of income, no education to speak of, no way to support Robbie nor make a home for him. Face it, Susan, when it comes to providing I win that one hands down and you know it. Have you got any goddamn idea how much it costs a month to keep this house afloat? How much your precious Robbie costs me in doctor bills every year? And your clothes? And your haircuts, nails, and your goddamn garden . . . Jesus! It never ends with you."

"*You would take Robbie away?*" Susan asked with tears in her eyes.

"*You belong to me, Susan. Don't ever forget that.*"

Jim pushed away the memory and opened the door, knowing that he'd been right all along. Susan belonged to him and he would get her back if he had to move heaven and earth.

Chapter Seven

Susan wore a tailored navy blue linen suit, navy shoes, and a matching purse when she went to apply for a job at Chili's Restaurant. The day manager, Alan Demerest, took one look at her and broke out into a very broad grin. "Have you ever waited tables before?"

"I'm a quick learner," Susan replied brightly.

"I'm sure you are." He smiled again.

"Is something wrong? You keep looking at me as if I have a spider crawling on my cheek or something."

"I'm sorry. It's just that you look more like a secretary than a waitress. I guess I've been in this business too long; I'm beginning to stereotype people, and that's not good."

Susan looked down at the shoes she'd so carefully chosen to match her suit. She wished she'd thought to match her skills to her wardrobe. Self-pity swooped across Susan's mind, but she batted it away. "I need the job."

"I wish I could help you out. I'm sure you'd be just great, but the truth of the matter is, when the colleges let out for

70

the summer we got flooded with applicants. I did my hiring two weeks ago. It's really tough out there for the kids graduating from school.''

"It's tough for everybody . . . out there," Susan said dejectedly.

Alan nodded. "Would you believe that out there on the floor right now I've got four college graduates and an MBA to tend bar? And you know what? They're happy as hell to have the jobs.''

"I would be, too," she said, choking back her emotions. She looked through the window in the door to the nonsmoking section of the restaurant. Two young waitresses whipped past the office bearing trays of steaming fajitas and baskets of chips and salsa. They looked crisp and professional in their white shirts and navy trousers. Susan had eaten in restaurants just like this one a thousand times in her life, never dreaming the day would come when she would envy them their jobs.

Alan's face softened. "Why don't you fill out one of our applications . . . in case we have an opening. We have a very good training program, opportunities for advancement, and a benefits package.''

Susan had never thought about waitressing as a career, but obviously other people had. She brightened a bit as Alan handed her a printed form. "Thanks.''

Alan ushered her to a quiet table in the bar area where she wouldn't be disturbed. Susan took one look at the form and realized she was again forced to lie. She wrote down her false name; correct address now that she had one; the telephone number of the manager's office that Andie had given her; a false social security number and her correct age, race, and sex.

Susan's hand was shaking when she handed the form back to Alan and thanked him.

"Good luck, Ms. Kaiser.''

"Thank you.''

Susan walked out of the restaurant and into the hot June sunshine. There was no sidewalk and her high heels kept sticking in the grass as she wove her way around driveways, parking lots, and gas station entrances. She felt horrendously conspicuous in her navy suit, which was gathering dust from the constant flow of heavy traffic. At the next corner she spied a Burger King, went inside, and found a pay phone. She bought a diet Coke and exchanged a five-dollar bill for quarters and began telephoning every restaurant in the area to inquire about employment. An hour later Susan was out of quarters and still hadn't found a job. She walked out of the Burger King and caught a bus that would take her to Kuy-kendahl, where she would have to walk the remainder of the way home. At the last gas station before she reached the apartment complex she bought a copy of the *Houston Post*.

Susan felt as if she were melting in the hot sun. She was used to high humidity in New Orleans, but it wasn't until that afternoon, after she'd walked nearly eight miles in high heels, that she realized that, since she was sixteen years old, Susan had driven an air-conditioned car nearly everywhere she went. She had a greater appreciation than ever for the comforts money could buy.

Susan went directly to Andie's office, since she had offered to watch Robbie while Susan was job hunting. Andie was on the phone when she opened the door and peeked her head around the corner. Andie waved her in and held up her index finger, indicating that she would only be a moment longer. "Thanks a bunch. Bye-bye."

Susan looked around the office. "Where's R—" Susan caught herself quickly—"Max?"

"At the pool. I felt sorry for him, staying cooped up in here when it was so nice outside."

Susan stood immediately, maternal alarm bells clanging.

Andie smiled. "He's fine. I was out there not three minutes ago, and Micaela is with him. They were chatting away when

I checked on them. He told Micaela he knew Spanish—''

"*Sesame Street,*" Susan interrupted with a smile.

"I never had kids; I wouldn't know. Anyway, I think he was learning quite a bit more today. So, how did it go, honey?"

"Not so good. It seems the high school and college kids have taken all the good jobs."

"I hadn't thought about it, but that's probably true." Andie stood. "Well, don't worry about it. Something will turn up."

You don't know the odds I'm up against, Susan thought to herself. "I'm sure it will." Susan tried to be cheerful, but, Lord, it was a strain. "I mustn't take up any more of your time. Thanks for looking after R—Max for me." Damn! It was more difficult to remember his name than her own.

Andie looked at her quizzically, then shrugged her shoulders and went back to work as Susan left the office.

Susan walked around the curving concrete path to the pool. The shade of the pine trees offered blessed relief from the sun. Susan opened the wooden gate to the pool area and scanned the water for Robbie.

The pool was filled to overflowing with children, a testimony to the fact that school was out for the summer.

A long line of young children stood waiting for their turn at the diving board. The shallow end was nearly unoccupied, since most of the children in the complex were older. What caught Susan's attention almost immediately was the fact that, rather than seeing doting young mothers near her age sunning themselves, she saw young men playing with their children.

Most of the children in the pool were Hispanic or Asian. She and Robbie were definitely the minority here. Susan put her hand over her eyes to shade them from the sun and to better search for Robbie. He wasn't in line for the diving board, nor was he in the water. She searched the lounge chairs and found Micaela. Sitting next to her, wearing a huge pair of fluorescent green swim trunks and black plastic sunglasses, with his arms crooked behind his head, was Robbie. His skin was glistening in the sun from an inch-thick coat of suntan oil. He looked like a miniature movie idol.

Susan was smiling when she walked up. "Max, isn't it? Could I have your autograph?"

Robbie craned his head around. "Mom, you're blocking my sun."

Susan stepped to the side, pulling up a plastic chair and sitting down. "Are you having a good time?"

"You bet. I always knew I wanted a swimming pool and I was right." He puffed out his chest and rubbed his belly. "This is the life."

Susan burst into laughter. "God, Max, what would I do without you?"

Micaela was wearing a fire-engine red one-piece bathing suit. She was a pretty girl, with long dark hair, round deep brown eyes, long lashes, and beautiful café-au-lait skin. She had told Susan she was nineteen and had been born in San Antonio, where she'd lived until moving to Houston. Micaela had known Luis since they were children and though they weren't married yet, Micaela knew someday they would be, "when we save up enough money." Micaela spoke with a very small accent, thanks to speech lessons she was taking two nights a week at Klein High School.

Micaela sat up and looked at Susan. "I hope you don' mind. He didn't have anything to do since Andie was so busy. And I thought the pool would be a good way for him to meet the other cheeldren . . . children."

"I love it here, Mom." Robbie sighed.

"I can see that."

"Did you find a job?" Robbie asked.

"No, I didn't. In fact, I'm very discouraged. Had we arrived three weeks ago, I wouldn't have had a problem at all. It seems I'm not qualified to do much. I can't type, I have no secretarial skills at all, I have no degree, no training for anything. The list of what I can't do is endless.'' The heat of the day, her aching feet, and her dispirited mood created stinging tears in Susan's eyes. She didn't want Robbie to see her crying, so she stood up and took off her suit jacket. ''I'll keep looking,'' she tried to assure Robbie. But look for what? she thought to herself.

''Can you clean a house?'' Micaela asked.

''Of course. I haven't done much else for the past eight years.''

''I work six days a week for a maid's service. Today is my day off; none of the girls want to work Saturdays and Sundays, so I'm always in demand. We had one of the girls quit two days ago because she's pregnant. Would you like the job?''

Susan couldn't believe she was nearly jubilant about a job as a housemaid, but she was. ''I'd love it.''

''I'll call Sandra and tell her about you before she gives the job to someone else,'' Micaela said as she rose and slipped her arms into a T-shirt.

''I can't thank you enough, Micaela,'' Susan said with a grateful smile.

''No problem,'' Micaela replied, her Spanish accent more pronounced.

After Micaela left Susan turned to Robbie. ''You look well done, young man. Maybe we should call it a day.''

Robbie took off his sunglasses. ''I guess so. I'll have to return all this stuff to Micaela.'' He sat on the edge of the chaise longue. ''She sure is nice, isn't she, Mom?''

''Yes. I think she's got best-friend potential.''

Robbie stood and slid his feet into a pair of man's-sized flip-flops. ''Too bad she's Luis's girlfriend.''

Susan put her hand on Robbie's shoulder as they walked around the pool to the pathway. ''Don't you think she's a little too old for you?''

Robbie looked at his mother aghast; then he broke out into a wide grin. "Naaaa." He laughed along with his mother.

That night Susan and Robbie were invited to Luis and Micaela's apartment for dinner. Susan welcomed the invitation, since she still didn't have silverware, kitchen tools, or cookware. She had given Andie some cash to pay for a burger and fries for Robbie's lunch. It wasn't until they walked into Micaela's apartment and smelled chicken frying that she realized she hadn't eaten a thing all day. Suddenly she was famished.

"Dinner is almost ready," Micaela said as Luis motioned to the glass-topped table and four gold velour and steel chairs in the dining area. "Have some chips and salsa while I finish the potatoes."

Robbie didn't waste a second as he grabbed a handful of the triangular-shaped corn chips. "This is really good," he said with his mouth full of salsa.

"I make it myself. Someday I'm going to sell my salsa and chips commercially."

Susan was instantly impressed. She picked up one of the chips and realized it was still warm. "You made these yourself?"

"*Sí* . . . yes."

"They're wonderful. Not greasy at all."

"No fat. I bake them instead of frying them."

Luis went to Micaela and kissed her cheek. "She's amazing, no?"

"Yes!" Robbie said, stuffing four more chips loaded down with fresh, tangy salsa into his mouth.

Susan tried to be as polite as possible, but her curiosity was killing her. "Micaela, did you get a chance to speak with Sandra?"

"Yes! She called me back right after I invited you to dinner. In fact, the phone was ringing when I walked in the door." She poured milk into the pan of boiled potatoes, added a half stick of butter, salt, and pepper and began mashing. "She told me to bring you with me tomorrow. You can have an interview, fill out the application, and then stay with me all day. She said she would see how it goes."

Concern creased Susan's brow.

"Don' worry." Luis patted her hand. "Micaela weel give you a good recommendation. She weel teech you everything about cleaning de houses."

Robbie got up from the table, his hunger satiated for the time being, and began investigating Micaela's domain. He went into the kitchen and asked if he could help, and Micaela gave him the silverware, which he placed correctly on the bright green placemats.

Micaela's apartment was truly a reflection of the girl herself. Her colors were bright and cheery and used with abandon rather than plan or formula. Everything from the cobalt blue and yellow Mexican pottery jars and plates on a bookshelf in the living room, to the red, green, and white floral sofa and love seat, and the new wooden coffee table, which Micaela had bought last month with her savings, was meticulously, spotlessly clean.

Robbie liked the bathroom, with its seashell-motif-border wallpaper, with shower curtain and towels to match. "Hey! This is cool stuff! Where'd you get it? WalMart?"

"Max! Must you always ask where people buy things?"

"I want to know. Besides, you said it was bad manners to ask how much it cost, not where it came from."

"Home Depot," Luis answered Max.

"Cool." Robbie peeked into the master bedroom and saw that Luis and Micaela owned his dream of dreams . . . a waterbed. "Aw, Mom! They have a waterbed! I've always wanted a waterbed." Then Robbie turned around and noticed a second bedroom. "Hey, cool! Another bedroom. Who sleeps in here?" Robbie had his hand on the doorknob when Luis seemed to appear out of nowhere.

"My office." He took Robbie's hand from the knob and walked him back down the short hall and through the living room to the dining room. "We're ready to eat," Luis announced.

Robbie was wide-eyed as Micaela placed a huge platter of fried chicken on the table, along with mashed potatoes, a tossed salad, and a bowl of green beans. Robbie thought he could eat every morsel all by himself.

Susan could never remember a time when her mouth drooled more. "This is a feast, Micaela. Thank you for inviting us," Susan said.

Micaela returned her smile. "You're welcome. Neighbors should help each other, no?" she said.

Susan thought of her neighborhood in New Orleans. They all lived such separated lives, sometimes not seeing each other for weeks or months on end. She knew most everyone's names, except for the newlywed couple who bought Pam and Ted's house, but she was certain that tonight no one knew she was gone and probably didn't care. Susan couldn't remember the last time one of her neighbors had invited her for dinner, and neither had Susan invited any of them to her home. Of course, because of Jim's drinking Susan had long ago abandoned home entertaining.

Susan was learning many things in her new life as Star, and though much of it was disheartening, there was a great deal to be said about this new set of eyes with which she viewed the world.

It was nine-thirty when Susan and Robbie went back to their own apartment. They'd had a wonderful time getting to know Luis and Micaela, but as Robbie got into bed that night, he couldn't help wondering what was in Luis's "office" that he didn't want Robbie to see.

Chapter Eight

Jim rammed his fist against the leather-wrapped steering wheel of his Mercedes. "Ow!" He placed his aching fist to his mouth, thinking he'd broken the skin. He rubbed it with his other hand. "Damn cops. I hate cops."

Jim Kidd had spent nearly three hours at police headquarters filling out paperwork, answering questions, and mostly defending himself. He couldn't believe how difficult it was to report someone missing. The cops had to call in shrinks, task-force consultants to the consultants, and God only knew who else, simply to determine that Susan was gone.

Sergeant Brian Patterson had been a nice enough fellow, a native New Orleanian, forty-two with two children of his own, but once Jim had filled out some very preliminary papers Patterson had handed Jim over to an investigator.

Lieutenant Roberts was as hard-boiled as they got, Jim determined from the minute he shook hands with the potbellied, balding man with the cigar in his mouth. Roberts spent half his time coughing and running his liver-spotted hand over his profusely sweating brow and the other half raking Jim over the coals, as if he had been the one who'd done something wrong.

"Look," Jim growled two hours into the grueling session, "Susan took off to who knows where with *my* son. I don't know where she is, how the hell she intends to stay away since she doesn't have any money . . ."

"I thought you said she took the car." Lieutenant Roberts picked up a sheet of paper containing his notes. "A Taurus, you said."

"That's right. A blue 1992 Taurus."

"Then she's got money."

"I don't get it."

Lieutenant Roberts looked over the rim of his reading glasses at Jim as if he were the dullest wit on the earth. "She could sell the car."

Jim was dumbfounded. Why hadn't he thought of that? He could hardly look the lieutenant in the eye, he felt so stupid. Suddenly Jim's memory bank deposited a scene of himself and Susan in their kitchen about three, maybe four months earlier. Jim had been shuffling through a sea of paperwork in those preliminary days of his negotiations with the Japanese. He hadn't known his head from his tail, he'd been so excited at the prospect of what this deal could mean to his career. He didn't realize it until now, but he'd completely blanked Susan and Robbie out of his existence. He'd lived and breathed, ate, slept, and drank this deal. Now, as he looked back on it, he remembered thinking that Susan was pressing him very hard for something, but he couldn't be bothered. He didn't care.

"What are these papers you want me to sign?"

"We talked about this a week ago and you agreed. I want my name to be on something around here. The house is in your name. The credit is in your name. The cars are both in your name. It's as if I don't exist. I'm just Mrs. James Kidd."

"So? What's the matter with that?"

"I want the Taurus in my name, and to do that you have to sign this transference of title."

"Jesus, Susan, is that all? Gimme the goddamn thing." He scribbled his signature on the line she indicated. *"Now, are we done with all this women's liberation shit? I've got a million things on my mind."*

Susan looked down at the slip of paper he'd signed. *"Me, too, Jim. Me, too."*

Jim slapped his hand to his forehead. "Damn! She was planning all this back then."

"Sorry, Mr. Kidd; I didn't hear you," Roberts said. "What about your wife?"

Jim blinked his tired eyes. He needed to get out of here and think this through. He needed a drink. He needed to calm down and get a grip. He couldn't tell the police the truth, that Susan left him because he'd hit her . . . twice. They'd laugh at him and never help him out. Shit. Could they put him in jail for assault and battery? Did they have to prove it first? Jim's ignorance of the law made him feel as if he were sitting on the hot seat. "My wife is a very happy woman. She would *not* run away. I think . . . she was abducted."

"There's a lot of sickos out there, Mr. Kidd, I'll grant you that, but we feel, given the evidence, that your wife may not have been all that happy. Did you ever receive any odd phone calls?"

"Odd?"

"Calls you couldn't explain. Calls from another man, perhaps?"

"You think my wife has a lover?" Jim threw himself back in the chair. "That's ludicrous."

"Not really. We see it all the time."

"I'll bet, but not with *my* wife. She has me."

Skepticism bordering on scorn riddled Lieutenant Roberts's

expression. "Did you argue with your wife, Mr. Kidd?"

"No. Never."

"Did she argue with you?"

"She nagged. Don't they all?"

"No. Do you take drugs, Mr. Kidd?"

"What kind of drugs?"

"The illegal kind . . . pot . . . coke . . . 'ludes . . . heroin . . . X?"

Jim kept shaking his head. "No. I don't do that kind of thing."

"You got a girlfriend, Mr. Kidd? Someone your wife might be jealous about?"

"God, no."

"Do you drink, Mr. Kidd?"

"Only socially."

Lieutenant Roberts lifted his head and looked Jim squarely in the eye. "Do you get drunk often? Maybe forget some of the things you say or do? You pass out at all? Have lapses of memory?"

"No. No. No. This is all a waste of time, I tell you. I want to know why you haven't dispatched your men to look for my wife!" With every word Jim's voice rose another octave and became more frantic.

"Did you ever hit your wife, Mr. Kidd?"

"No! Dammit! I never hit my wife . . . or my kid. I never did anything. But . . . I got pressures."

"We all do, Mr. Kidd."

The interrogation lasted another hour, but as far as Jim was concerned nothing was accomplished. Roberts had introduced Jim to a counselor, Loretta Pierce, who treated Jim as if he were Attila the Hun. She used the same questionnaire as Lieutenant Roberts, and Jim wondered if these people had any concept of the time they were wasting.

"I already answered that question."

"I'd just like to hear for myself," Loretta said placidly as she took notes on a yellow legal pad.

"I don't fight with my wife. I have never hit my wife, and if anybody says I did, they're goddamn liars. You know there's a lot of jealous people in the world, and plenty of them would like to trip me up."

"Is that so?"

"Yes. I make a very good living. Very good. I provide Susan . . . and Robbie, too, with the finest money can buy. How many seven-year-old kids do you know who've got a Pentium computer at home?"

"None, actually."

"Mine does."

"Is he good at it?"

"Who?"

"Your son. Is he proficient with the computer?"

"Yes . . . I think so. Yes. Very definitely. He's always got his face plastered next to the screen." Jim visualized Robbie sitting in his room in his little wooden chair at his kiddie table, playing games on the computer. Jim had brought the computer home from work as part of his year-end bonus eighteen months earlier. Jim wasn't exactly sure what Robbie did on the computer and assumed that he played games on it. He wasn't smart enough to figure out Windows, was he? Jim had never asked.

"That's wonderful that you encourage learning in this manner, Mr. Kidd."

"Thank you." Jim finally relaxed a bit, crossed his right leg over his left, and folded his hands in his lap.

"If you and your wife didn't quarrel, Mr. Kidd, what other reason could you give for her disappearance?"

"I . . . I don't know."

Loretta lifted her chin and looked at him with dark, knowing eyes, as if she'd heard his response before . . . many, many times. "What I meant was, perhaps she quarreled with

83

her parents, a brother, a sister, your family . . ."

"No . . . Not my family. No," Jim answered tersely and a bit too quickly. "Susan doesn't know my family."

"They don't live here?"

"No. But her family does. Susan is an only child, but now that you mention it that could be a possibility. Susan hasn't gotten along with her parents since we met. Well, actually, since Susan got pregnant with Robbie . . ."

"He's not your son?"

"Of course he is. Why did you ask that?"

"Just the way you answered . . . as if Susan got pregnant by herself."

"Well, I certainly didn't mean it that way."

"I see." Loretta scribbled a few more notes to herself. "She was pregnant before you married her."

"Yes. She was a freshman at Tulane. I was a senior."

Loretta looked at the first page of notes. She smiled winningly at him, though Jim detected a bit of condescension. Maybe he was becoming paranoid.

"Mr. Kidd . . . Jim Kidd. Not *the* Jim Kidd? The same Jim Kidd who made that incredible touchdown against SMU back in . . ."

"Nineteen-eighty-five! That was me!" Jim grinned at Loretta. "Hell of a game. I never would have guessed you for a football fan."

"I graduated in 1967. I get season tickets every year."

"That's great. Just great."

Loretta stood up and shook Jim's hand warmly. "Thank you, Mr. Kidd, and let me assure you that we will do everything in our power to find your wife and little boy," she said and walked away.

Jim did not see the change in Loretta's expression as she walked away, nor the last note she scribbled on her pad: Check college record. ABC Act. DWIs. Neighbor complaints. Loretta circled the word "abuse."

*   *   *

When Jim left he promised Lieutenant Roberts that he would bring in more pictures of Susan and Robbie and would report any correspondence or communication that occurred between them should he hear from his wife and son.

The police were as ineffectual as he knew they would be, Jim thought to himself as he drove home. Tied down with all that paperwork and red tape, legalities and rules, it was a wonder they could issue traffic tickets.

As he drove home on I-10, Jim realized that the only way he was ever going to find Susan was to hunt her down himself. "Not an easy task, old man," he said to himself.

He had more obligations at the office now than ever before. If he put in sixteen hours a day, it still wouldn't be enough. His Japanese deal had turned into a dragon, devouring time, manpower, and attention. Tomorrow morning a new assistant would be assigned to him in order that the work be expedited.

Jim didn't know which way to turn. He couldn't walk out of the office at such a crucial time to go traipsing around Louisiana to find Susan. He had worked too hard for too long to blow it all now over a . . . what had the cops called it? . . . "domestic problem."

He would have to hire someone to find Susan. A private investigator was what he needed. Then he could keep up his momentum at work and get Susan back home where she belonged without involving the police any more than necessary.

Why hadn't he thought of it earlier? Yes. That was what needed to be done. Jim didn't like the way the police spoke to him, slipping insinuations that he was some kind of demon into every question and comment. He'd like to see how many guys could stand up to that kind of drilling. Damn! He knew guys who did a lot worse than he had when they had to let off a little steam. Jim wasn't a bad guy, but he could see how the cops could make it look that way.

It was best for all concerned that Jim keep the police out of his life. Definitely best.

Chapter Nine

Sandra Tree, of the prominent and illustrious Philadelphia Tree family by marriage, and then retaining the name after her divorce, welcomed Susan to her sunny offices off Louetta Road in Spring, Texas.

Sandra, dark haired and strikingly attractive, was smartly dressed in a conservative white linen summer suit with a yellow silk blouse. Sandra's office looked as if it had been the model in a decorating magazine, Susan thought as she sat in a cozy chair upholstered in an English tea rose print in soft greens and pinks. Sandra's desk was a light pickled Country French writing desk containing all the newest office equipment and computers that frightened Susan more than she wanted to admit.

Sandra looked to be the same age as Susan, which made Susan uncomfortable. Sandra was incredibly efficient, as she answered her calls, sent a Fax, redialed a client's house, and double-checked the computer log for an update on the woman's account.

Finally Sandra turned toward Susan. "I'm sorry for the interruptions, but when Angela quit my schedule got thrown off. You, my dear, are a blessing in disguise."

"Thank you."

Sandra shoved up the sleeves of her jacket to reveal a very expensive gold watch. She turned to the computer and poised her hands above the keyboard. "Now, let's get the vital statistics as quickly as possible so we won't delay Micaela any more than necessary. Name?"

"Star Kaiser."

Sandra threw Susan a suspicious look but continued with her questioning. Susan ran through her litany of lies, until all the blanks on the screen were filled. Sandra punched the EN-TER button and turned back to Susan.

"Micaela has gone to find you one of our uniforms for today. If you like the work, I'll order your proper size. All my girls are bonded and insured. At Merry Maids we pride ourselves on efficiency and thoroughness. You are hired to clean, not rearrange someone's house, so don't let them buffalo you into thinking you should do more. All our clients have a list of what we do and don't do. Report any breakages of anything—even appliances—to me, so that I can contact the client. We run teams of two or three girls to a house, so you will never be alone. No sexual harassment will be tolerated from male or female clients. Some of my girls are still learning English, so I would advise learning a bit of Spanish yourself. I speak it fluently; it can't hurt. You will be paid by check twice a month on the first and the fifteenth. I provide workman's comp but not health insurance. However, there is a company plan available if you choose to join for forty-five dollars a month. Do you have a child?"

"Yes. Max is seven."

"It's another ten dollars to cover him."

"I'll think about that. Right now I need the money." Susan knew she didn't dare sign up for insurance because that would be another set of lies, papers that could track her down, another chance for her false Social Security Number to be flagged. She needed to tread lightly. "I was wondering . . . could I possibly be paid in cash?"

Sandra's perfectly arched dark eyebrow lifted. "I usually expect that question from one of my Mexican girls . . . especially the ones who look illegal."

"I'm not an illegal alien."

Sandra's expression softened as her eyes filled with concern. "Are you sure you want this job? You aren't exactly the maid type. . . ."

"I need this job . . . desperately."

Sandra suddenly felt the pangs of Susan's dilemma. "I knew that the minute you walked in the door. Who hit you?"

Susan rolled her eyes upward so that Sandra wouldn't see her fear. "Am I so transparent?"

"I'm a woman, Star. We all know when one of us is in trouble. I could use some help here in the office. None of my girls have any skills. . . ."

"Neither do I. But I can clean rings around anyone."

Sandra smiled broadly. "Wanna bet? These girls are miracle workers." She laughed. "Okay. For now, you can learn what they know. And I'll see what I can do about paying you in cash, but just for a while. My accountant is a stickler for this kind of thing, and the feds watch me like a hawk. These girls are forever trying to bring their sisters, aunts, and mothers across the border."

"I had no idea," Susan said. "But thank you for all your help."

Just then Micaela knocked on the door and peeked her head inside. "Are you ready?"

Susan was smiling. "Yes." She shook hands with Sandra and left the office.

When the door closed Sandra whispered to herself, "Poor thing. Thank God I don't have to walk in her shoes."

Becoming

* * *

Susan wore a white uniform with powder-blue lettering on the breast pocket that said MERRY MAIDS and was encircled with stars, hearts, crescent moons, and balloons. Micaela, Susan, and Juanita rode in a white Chevette emblazoned with the company logo to the west side of Houston, where they were to clean two houses that day in an elegant subdivision.

The first house was in Barker's Landing and was the home of a chiropracter, his wife, and their one-and-a-half-year-old son. When they walked through the leaded glass and wood door Susan thought she'd walked into a mansion. The three girls walked across the beige-tiled foyer, under the sweeping circular staircase and the triple-tiered brass chandelier to a two-story living room elegantly appointed in deep, rich burgundy brocades and black silks. A massive red brick fireplace soared to the ceiling and opened into both the living room and the adjacent, sunny family room. The mistress of the house, Gaye, had raced across the room to retrieve her baby son from the interior of the fireplace.

"Bucky! Just look at you!" she said, brushing off a head-to-toe covering of soot and ashes as the child squealed in delight. She turned to the maids. "Obviously I need the fireplace cleaned out as well. Just add it to my bill," she said with exasperation as she led her son off to the bathroom for a bath.

Susan couldn't help giggling to herself. How many times had she gone through the same kind of experience with Robbie? However, Micaela and Juanita didn't miss a beat. Juanita was already out the door and unloading cleaning supplies, mops, brooms, and the vacuum from the car.

"We bring our own vacuum, but in a house this size, we use the client's vacuums and mops, too. It makes it go faster. Today you start in the living room. Juanita does the kitchen. They are her specialty and that's all she does. You and I can clean nearly the whole house in the time it takes her to do that one room.''

''She's that slow?''

''No, there's just more to do in the kitchen. Especially if the client has paid extra to clean out the refrigerator.''

Susan looked up the huge staircase and at the vast master's wing to the left. ''I don't know.'' Susan was instantly aware that even her parents' house wasn't this big.

''You'll be fine. You start upstairs and change the sheets in the bedroom and nursery. Gaye leaves out clean sheets for us to put on. We are not responsible for doing the laundry, but I always start the washer for her. Upstairs is her husband's study, and all you have to do is dust and vacuum. It's the staircase and two baths up there that take the time. I'll start on the fireplace before the baby gets out of the bath.''

''Good idea.''

Juanita distributed three plastic trays, each filled with the appropriate cleaners, cloths, sponges, and brushes. There were special polishes for chrome, brass, and gold fixtures. Tiny brushes were to be used with the mildew cleaners. Steel-wool soap pads and a special calcium remover were used on shower doors, toilets, baths, and sinks.

No wonder these girls worked miracles, Susan thought as she followed Micaela's instructions and procedures. Every task was to be accomplished in a precise order, with no deviations allowed. Because of her past experience as a housewife Susan had misgivings about the enormity of their task, given that they were only allotted three and a half hours. It wasn't until she was an hour into her chores that Susan realized how different this work was. Since this was not her home she never had to answer the phone or the door, make lunch for her son, run errands, or begin preparations for the family dinner, all of which she noticed that Gaye was doing while the girls cleaned.

The house was spotless and fresh-smelling when they finished, collected a check from Gaye, and returned to their automobile. Micaela started the engine.

"You did very well, Susan, and we finished thirty minutes ahead of schedule. We have time to get a hamburger before we go to the next house."

Juanita's arms were folded across her chest. "She dint dry de sinks in de batrooms. I had to do eet."

"I'll do better next time," Susan assured her.

"Okay." Juanita smiled.

They drove through Two Pesos for tacos and diet Cokes. Juanita didn't know as much English as Micaela did, so the two girls spoke Spanish to each other a good deal. Sandra is right, Susan thought to herself as she munched on the taco, I need to take Spanish lessons.

"These tacos are great!" Susan said.

"Dey are sheet!" Juanita said with a scowl. "Micaela could make theem bayter."

"I could. And I'm going to. I wonder . . ." Micaela looked up at the huge sign with the logo on it. Then she lifted her paper cup filled with ice and diet Coke. She pointed to the bottom of the cup. "Just as I thought. Here's the company address. I'll write to the president and ask them to try my salsa." Micaela took out a ballpoint pen and scribbled the address on a piece of paper and stuck them both back in her purse. "I'm practically in business already!"

"You're really serious about marketing your own salsa?"

Micaela looked at Susan in the rearview mirror. "You don't think I want to be a maid all my life, do you?"

"I . . . thought . . ."

"No way. I'm only doin' this until I save enough money to start my business."

"What does Luis think about this?" Susan inquired.

Juanita started laughing. "Who cares?"

Micaela and Susan began laughing with her. "Who

cares?'' Micaela shrugged her shoulders. ''Men . . . they come . . . they go. . . . You gotta take care of yourself first. No?''

''Yes,'' Susan said as they finished their lunch, deposited their waste paper in the paper bag, and headed for the next assignment.

Susan was beside herself with wonder. Micaela was almost eight years younger and she knew more about life than Susan ever hoped to learn. God! How right she was! Not since the day she'd been watching that women's talk show with the panel of psychiatrists discussing alcoholism and the dependency of wives had Susan had such a revelation about the inadequacies of her upbringing.

Susan had been duped by her mother's fantasies for her and a worn-out Southern cultural code of ethics that declared that a woman was meant to subject her mind, body, and life to a man the day she married. Susan's frame of reference came from her mother, who was raised by Grandmother Alecia—in Susan's estimation, the quintessential Southern lady.

To grow up in Susan's world of Old New Orleanian values and mores was to step back a hundred and fifty years. Susan had attended private girls' schools all her life. She barely knew what boys thought or dreamed or acted like. She had no brothers, not even any boy cousins. Even in her neighborhood there were only three boys to eleven girls. The boys were transported by their nonworking mothers to and from piano or horn lessons, tennis, golf, and swimming lessons. They all belonged to the same clubs and their parents entertained each other at crab boils and fish frys in each others' homes.

Like her mother, Susan had believed that when she married her husband would love her and care for her all her life. Perhaps if she'd gone out-of-state to college, her life might have had more illumination, but she'd simply taken classes at Tulane and lived at home.

It wasn't until Susan was married and taking care of Robbie that she began watching television talk shows and heard stories of suffering that other women in places far removed from New Orleans underwent. Susan could remember watching with detachment as the women on television cried or raged at the injustices they'd endured. For a long time Susan actually had believed these women had fabricated these stories in order to see themselves on *Oprah!* or *Phil Donahue*.

Susan believed that her own hard-luck experience of getting pregnant with Robbie during the first two months of dating Jim was as shameful an event as anything these women spoke about. But Jim had married her, which washed away her sin. Or had that simply swept it under the table?

Jim had resented the baby, but he'd wanted to marry Susan. If she were brutally honest with herself, she would have to admit that Jim wanted to be Bart Beaulieu's son-in-law more than he'd wanted to be Susan's husband. My God! she thought. Where had that revelation come from? She didn't want to think so little of herself . . . but Jim did.

Susan chose not to reflect upon her parents' scorn, because it was too painful. She didn't want to remember things or times that weren't "nice." And Susan was a nice girl. She had pushed away the memories of those days so successfully that she had convinced herself they had never happened.

She realized she'd been walking through her life in a coma. Jim had used liquor to anesthetize himself, but Susan used denial. For the first time she saw the parallel between herself and Jim. No wonder they'd stayed together as long as they had. In a twisted way they had needed each other.

Suddenly the car pulled to a stop in front of a beautiful two-story colonial house. Susan was so lost in her thoughts, she had not realized Micaela was talking to her.

"Hey, gringa," Micaela teased. "Let's see how fast you

can move. If we finish early, we'll make that call to the president of Two Pesos.''

Susan crawled out of the small backseat and took the mops and brooms Micaela handed her. ''Just call me 'Speedy.' ''

As they went up the brick walkway to the front door, Susan realized that the difference between herself and the young Mexican girl was that Susan was afraid of living—she just wanted to get through life and be done with it—and Micaela was afraid she'd die before she'd grasped all she could out of living. It was strange that Susan's life had taken such an odd turn and yet, in the midst of this whirlwind, she was learning more about herself, more about life, than she'd ever dreamed possible.

Chapter Ten

New Orleans

It took Jim three days to drum up the courage to tell his business associates that Susan and Robbie were missing. The questions they asked were more probing than those of the police, and only half as sympathetic.

"I'm sorry to hear that, Jim. Guess you've been working too much lately, huh, ol' pal?" James stated.

"Gee, that's a shame, Jim. I caught a lot of flack at home, too. Jesus, Jim, haven't you learned yet how to appease your wife?" Bob Jones said.

"I'll bet she's got a boyfriend. They all do," Elliot in accounting said morosely. Jim knew that Betty had left Elliot three years ago for another guy, and Elliot was still in shock. Frankly, Jim couldn't blame Betty. In Jim's estimation Elliot had the personality of a handful of dead rats.

Other guys with other problems had never interested Jim. He was always too busy to hear about their wives, their bills, their kids. "Like nobody else had the same problems anyway," Jim thought to himself at the time.

However, no one could recommend a private detective. Jim played tennis every Tuesday and Thursday night when he wasn't plowed under with work, so he asked some of the guys at the tennis club if they knew of anyone who could help him find Susan. He was met with condescending looks and polite replies to the negative. It wasn't until he was sitting at the bar having a post-match beer with Simon Hebert that he learned anything helpful.

"Ah know of a guy. Ah had to use him in a personal-injury law suit about a year ago. Ah never met him, but he was fast and good. As Ah recall, he took less than ten days to find the missing witness to the accident," Simon told Jim with a pronounced Southern drawl.

"That's great! Where is this guy?"

"Here in Nawleans," Simon replied. "Lemmah see . . . his name is, let's see . . . Rawlings, Tate Rawlings."

"This is great, Simon. I'll give him a call."

Simon finished his beer, tied his white *v*-necked, long-sleeved tennis sweater around his suntanned neck, and picked up his racket. "Ah have anothah match. See you latah, Jim. Good luck."

Still knee-deep in contract negotiations with the Japanese, it was a full week before Jim found the time to place a call to Tate Rawlings, private investigator. His secretary informed Jim that it would be another ten days before Mr. Rawlings had an opening.

"But she's been gone for ten days already! This is an emergency."

"They all are, Mr. Kidd. How about Monday, July eighth, at three o'clock, and if there's a cancellation, I'll call you."

"I guess I'll have to take it," Jim replied. "Tell me—is he that good?"

"He's that good. We'll see you on Monday the eighth at three."

Jim slammed down the receiver. "Goddammit . . . this guy is worse than the police!" Jim looked at his desk, which was piled with paperwork and a Daytimer filled with back-to-back meetings for the next four days solid. "Shit. It's not like I don't have enough to worry about without Susan pulling this crap on me."

Jim's assistant, Tiffany Derring, knocked on his door and then opened it. "You're wanted in the conference room, Mr. Kidd," she said, pushing back an errant lock of dishwater blond hair from her narrow forehead. Of all the people in the world who didn't fit their name, Tiffany was the best example. Tiffany had learned at an early age that if she wanted to be a diamond and not a rhinestone, she would have to develop her talents; there wasn't enough makeup in the world to change her homely face into anything other than what it was. When Tiffany had started out in the business world she had intended to become the best secretary in New Orleans.

After two weeks at Metro Media Tiffany knew that her lot in life was to be a great deal more than somebody's gofer. Tiffany wanted Jim Kidd's job, and she didn't care how many hours it took, how many years in school, how many lost weekends. She was going to learn everything he knew and then some. Now that she had been with Metro Media five years, Tiffany was more confident than ever that she would have Jim's job someday if she never took another class at LSU. Jim was a drunk. It was only a matter of time before everyone else figured it out. The fact that he had pulled off this Japanese deal was a blessing in disguise. Jim was a great pitchman and an even better salesman, but he fell apart on the details; the legalities, the business plans, the contracts. Tiffany had covered his rear for years. At the first of the year she'd been promoted to assistant manager, which meant that

her name went next to Jim's on every contract, every letter
and memo his office put out.

Tiffany was on her way to the top.

Jim looked at his watch. "How can it possibly be eleven
o'clock already? I haven't finished that report . . ." He shuf-
fled through the stack of reports and memos on his cluttered
desk.

"It's okay. I inputted all your changes this morning, finished up your conclusions, made copies, and put them in the
conference room."

Jim sighed with relief. "God, we make a good team, don't
we?"

"The best, sir." Tiffany smiled, revealing her crooked
teeth. Tiffany allowed Jim to believe she took her subservient
role seriously; he was the kind of man who didn't understand
anything else.

When Jim walked past Tiffany she could still smell last
night's bourbon on his breath. She followed him down the
hall, thinking that he couldn't keep up this killer pace and the
drinking forever. All the signs are there, she thought to herself. Even Susan wasn't sticking around for his downfall.

Houston

Susan woke up with a smile on her face. She stretched out
and then kissed Robbie's cheek. "Wake up, pumpkin. It's a
new day."

Susan nearly sprang out of bed and hummed a tune as she
walked into the bathroom and started her shower. Robbie
rolled over sleepily and slapped his hand over the clock radio,
dreamily thinking the music he heard was coming from it.

"Uh, it's Mommy." He rolled back over and closed his
eyes again.

Susan showered quickly, washed her short dark hair, then
toweled herself dry and put on her uniform. As she dried her

hair with the blower, she couldn't help looking at the happy, pretty girl in the mirror.

It was downright weird how she could be so happy cleaning houses, living in a cramped apartment with hardly any furniture and no car. She guessed she liked her work so much because it was all so new. "The honeymoon period" was what Sandra had called it, but Susan knew it was more than that.

Susan was free for the first time in her life. With her false identity she was suspended between reality and illusion. Separated from Jim, she was able to see how deeply disturbed she'd been. She could look back on her life in New Orleans as if it had happened to someone else. And oddly, Susan felt pity for that girl. Susan also knew she never wanted to be that woman again.

Susan believed she'd made the right decision for herself and for Robbie. They had made new friends in Houston; people who liked her for who she was and not because she was Jim Kidd's wife or Bart Beaulieu's daughter. She was in the process of teaching herself to speak her mind, a practice Jim had stifled from the very beginning of their life together. This rash and possibly irrational act of running away had taught her that she knew nothing about life, relationships, or the working woman she had now become. Day care, job sharing, maternity benefits, taxes, Social Security, and workman's compensation had all previously been just words to Susan. But to Star Kaiser they were lifelines to security.

To Susan Beaulieu *security* had meant being married. To Susan Kidd security was keeping Jim sober. She knew now that she could never rely on a man, or any other person, to give her security. She had to do it for herself.

Susan finished putting on her makeup. She went to the kitchen and boiled water for a cup of instant coffee. "Robbie, are you up? I only have twenty minutes before Micaela will be ready to leave."

Robbie was rubbing his eyes as he walked into the kitchen. He looked taller, Susan thought as she hugged her son. Or was he thinner? "Good morning, pumpkin."

"Mornin'." He crawled onto one of the two mismatched wooden chairs they'd found in the storage building. Andie had lent them a foldaway card table. Robbie picked up his spoon and yawned. "Can I have Cocoa Puffs?"

Susan rolled her eyes. "I didn't buy cereal yesterday."

"Aw, Mom! You promised."

"I was too tired to shop after working all day. Today at noon I'll get you something. How about Cheerios instead?"

"Okay," he said and waited while Susan filled a bowl with cereal and milk, then placed it before him. "Thanks."

"I forgot to tell you that you won't be going to Luis's today."

"Why not?"

"Because Andie found a new girl, Toni Camelo, who baby-sits."

"Aw, gees. Do I havta? I have a good time with Luis. He's got a Sega."

"Joy."

"I don't want to spend all day with a bunch of babies." He angrily shoved a heaping spoonful of cereal into his mouth.

"Toni Camelo is certified by the state to watch children. She's got the meeting room downstairs; you can still swim with the older kids. You'll see, it will be fine."

"What's the matter with Luis?"

"Luis and Micaela were helping us out for the short term, until we got settled. Micaela says that Luis needs his privacy to get his work done. Whatever that means."

"He makes things in his office."

"What kind of things?"

Robbie shrugged his shoulders. "I dunno. He won't let me in there."

Susan looked at the clock. "Omigosh! I'll be late."

While Susan rushed to slap together a peanut butter sandwich for her lunch, Robbie shoveled his cereal into his mouth, then raced to the bedroom for a pair of shorts, a T-shirt, and tennis shoes. He'd started out of the room when he remembered his new bathing trunks, sunglasses, and his own key to the apartment, which he attached to his shorts with a large safety pin.

Susan took Robbie down to the meeting room where Toni Camelo would be caring for seven children. She was about thirty-five, short, and as round as a roly-poly doll. She had a merry face with deepset green eyes and a wide smile. Toni was holding a screaming two-year-old boy whose mother had just left, while a three-year-old girl and a four-year-old boy tugged on her pants leg, asking for drinks and cookies. Two six-year-old girls sat off to the side of the room at a children's plastic picnic table with coloring books, crayons, scissors, and glue. The redheaded little girl picked her nose and watched Robbie intently as he came into the room.

Susan introduced herself and Robbie quickly and then turned to leave. Robbie walked with her to the sliding glass doors.

"Now, you be good for Toni." Susan kissed him.

"Don't worry, Mom." He motioned behind him with his thumb. "She looks as if she could use all the help she can get."

"She does have her hands full."

Robbie puffed out his chest. "I'll take care of things here until you get back."

"Okay, honey." Susan kissed him again and walked away. She turned back to take a last look at Robbie, thinking he'd still be standing at the door, a forlorn expression on his face. However, he was gone, and through the glass she saw him walking over to Toni, taking the hands of the two children at her leg, and walking with them to a pile of building blocks.

Susan, like Robbie, had not a minute to waste on sentiment. She dashed around to the parking lot in time to see Juanita and Micaela driving up in the company car. Susan got in and they drove east to I-45 and then north to the Woodlands, where they spent every Wednesday and Thursday cleaning houses.

New Orleans

Lieutenant Roberts rubbed the bald spot on his head as he looked at the newest report on the Susan Kidd case. He looked up from his desk to the blue-uniformed man sitting next to him. "You took this call?"

"Yes, sir."

"Get this State Trooper . . . Mulday, on the phone for me."

"Yes, sir," Officer Barnett replied as he left the office, went back to his desk, and placed the series of long-distance calls it took to track down this first sighting of Susan Kidd.

Forty minutes later, Roberts picked up the phone receiver and spoke to Mulday.

"I read your report and I wanted to verify some points with you."

"Fine," Mulday said from his car phone.

"You state here that there was a child with her."

"Yes, that's right. A boy, about six to eight. He matched the description and APB photo. As did Mrs. Kidd."

"You also state here that Mrs. Kidd had a bruised face. Is that accurate?"

"Yes. Swollen jaw, bruise. Her eye was bloodshot, and not just from crying. It's a wonder her jaw wasn't busted. Somebody decked her good."

"Are you aware that her husband claims they have never exchanged words? Never fought? He has never hit her?"

"I heard words to that effect from someone in your office . . . a Mrs. Loretta Pierce." Trooper Mulday paused. "Listen,

Lieutenant Roberts, we have a word up here in Baton Rouge for what that lady's husband told you . . . bullshit. Off the record, I hope this woman is one of the few who can find a way to beat our system. I hope to hell she finds a way to fall through the cracks and never come out. To tell you the truth, I haven't been able to get her out of my mind. You know?''

"Yeah, I know."

"She sure was pretty. And that little boy of hers . . . he was precious. They were sittin' ducks where I found 'em. If I was that woman's big brother, I'd knock the shit out of anyone who did something like that to her."

Roberts looked down at the family photographs Jim Kidd had sent him. He knew just what Trooper Mulday was saying. As old as he was, as seasoned and cynical as he'd become, this case had gotten under his skin, too. "You have no bead on where she went after you left her?"

"No. And frankly, I can't say I'd tell you if I did."

"Need I remind you—"

"No, you need not." Mulday expelled a rush of air. "No one in this area has spotted her license plate since that night."

"Very well. Thank you."

"No problem, Lieutenant Roberts."

Roberts took four calls, all of which had been waiting for him while he'd spoken with Mulday. A frantic mother needed to be calmed when she'd come home at noon and found a note from her very angry sixteen-year-old daughter, who had run away to Los Angeles. Roberts knew that if they didn't find the girl before she hit L.A., it might take months to find her and, when they did, there was no telling what would have happened to her. More than likely she'd be on the streets. Roberts had dedicated his life to finding missing and lost persons. As the years passed the stories had blended together, becoming one hideous human nightmare.

He'd been only twenty-three when he'd started this job in 1950. Now he was sixty-eight, three years over retirement age, but he was the best in his field, and the force would keep him as long as he wanted to stay on. In the beginning Roberts had believed he was doing the altruistic "right" thing in bringing runaways back home. Now he knew better.

People ran away from pain, from intolerable situations, and from lives they could no longer control. Susan Kidd was running from a husband who beat her. She was afraid, and yet he knew that she, like all the others, was courageous and, yes, a bit foolhardy, to risk everything she had to find a new life.

Roberts thought that eventually they would find Susan, though people often managed to stay lost. He'd learned over twenty years ago that simply bringing people back home wasn't the answer. The home had to change and until it did, Roberts knew he couldn't justify his place on this earth if he didn't spend as much time with the abusers as he did hunting the abused.

Chapter Eleven

New Orleans

Bart Beaulieu was sitting on the back porch in a wicker rocking chair under a ceiling fan, dressed in white summer slacks and a soft yellow golf shirt that set off his tanned, handsome face, when Effie, the maid, announced Lieutenant Roberts's arrival. At fifty-five Bart was still athletically built, due to his Saturday golf games and the Sunday tennis matches on his home courts.

Roberts shook Bart's hand. "Thank you for honoring my request to come out here. It's just that . . . well, Mrs. Beaulieu and I would rather not have our family's business discussed in front of strangers."

"It's not a problem," Roberts replied, already feeling sticky in his armpits—and it wasn't from the heat.

"Won't you please sit down, Lieutenant?" Bart motioned to a black-and-white-striped, canvas-cushioned wicker chair next to the rocker. "Perhaps Effie could bring you some iced tea."

"That'd be fine." Roberts sat in the chair directly under the rotating fan. "Will Mrs. Beaulieu be joining us?"

"She's been indisposed since Susan . . . this incident. She may join us later."

"It's important that I have her input also. I could come back . . ."

"Very well, if it's that important."

"Yes, it is."

"When Effie returns with our tea I'll have her bring Annette down."

Lieutenant Roberts nodded.

Bart crossed his legs and leaned toward Roberts. "What can you tell me about my daughter's disappearance?" Bart asked sincerely.

"Not much more than you already know, I'm afraid. I wanted this meeting with you so I could draw a more accurate picture of Susan and her life."

"What on earth for?" Bart's silver eyebrow lifted in surprise.

Just then the maid returned with tall, cut-crystal glasses of iced tea decorated with paper-thin lemon rings and sprigs of fresh mint. Roberts drank deeply of the refreshing, perfectly sweetened tea. "That's the best tea I've had in years." He smiled at the maid.

"Could you ask Mrs. Beaulieu to join us, please? And when you return bring us the pitcher of tea for Lieutenant Roberts," Bart requested as he turned back to the policeman.

"As I was saying . . . In cases like this anything you can tell me will be of value. The more I know about Susan and Robbie, the better I'll be able to solve this case."

"Of course. I'll do anything. I just want my little girl back."

Roberts took a small notebook and pen out of his shirt

pocket. When he pulled back the cover he noticed that the pages were damp from his own perspiration. He glanced up at Bart, who still looked as if he were cool as ice. Roberts jotted down the words *little girl.*

"What are you writing? I haven't said anything yet."

"Oh, I'm just making note that you have agreed to cooperate. Legalities. You can never be too careful."

Bart smiled knowingly. "I understand."

I doubt it, Roberts thought to himself.

Just then Annette Beaulieu walked through the French doors. She was a stunningly beautiful blue-eyed woman with cool, aristocratic bones and an elegant carriage. She looked to be in her late forties. Annette wore her silvery blond hair in a perfectly executed French twist with a tiny wisp of bangs across her smooth forehead. She was dressed in a sheer silk full-skirted floral dress in turquoise and blue, and there were tasteful pearls set in gold mountings on her ears and an expensive gold rope around her neck.

Roberts thought he was seeing an angel.

She walked across the porch, sat in a chair next to her husband, and took the glass of tea the maid offered her. Though she wore concern on her face, she wasn't as indisposed as Bart had led the lieutenant to believe. Roberts had been expecting a highly distraught woman with puffy eyes and shaking hands. This woman looked to be none of those things.

"I hope you're feeling better, my dear," Bart said, patting Annette's hand.

"Somewhat." She tossed him the concession. She turned to Roberts, ignoring the adoration in his eyes. "Do I understand correctly that you have news of Susan?"

"Yes, ma'am. We've received a report that from New Orleans she went to Baton Rouge. She was spotted on the side of Highway 12 by a state trooper. She had been sleeping in her car, and the trooper told her to leave."

"Why did he do that? Why didn't he tell her to come home?"

"Mrs. Beaulieu, ma'am, at that time there had been no missing person's report. Had the officer not asked her to move on she could have been in danger. For a woman to be all alone like that on the side of the road . . . Well, ma'am, she's damn lucky that trooper didn't find her dead."

"Oh, God." Annette's hand fluttered to her throat. Suddenly she lost her composure. The calm on her face shattered in an instant. "Why would Susan do this to us?"

"Do what, ma'am?" Roberts made another note.

"Put us through all this. Surely she knew we would worry. Surely she knows we're waiting for a phone call, anything from her. What is the matter with that girl? My God, didn't I raise her with better manners than this?" Annette's eyes flew from Roberts to Bart and back to Roberts again.

Roberts shook his head. "I seriously doubt you have crossed her mind once in the past several weeks. Perhaps even months."

"What are you saying?" Annette's voice was strained.

Bart was indignant. "We're her family."

Roberts's old, cynical eyes took in a great deal as he watched the reactions between Bart and Annette. "The state trooper who found her stated that she'd been badly beaten."

Annette covered her face with her hands. Her entire body was shaking. "God, this isn't happening. Not to my baby . . ." she shrieked.

"Effie!" Bart yelled for the maid. "Effie, hurry."

The maid came rushing onto the porch.

"Take Mrs. Beaulieu upstairs and get her another Valium."

Bart helped Annette out of her chair and handed her over to Effie's care. "You'll be fine, my dear. I'll finish with Lieutenant Roberts and then I'll be up to see you."

As soon as the two women left, Bart turned back to Roberts. "Is this true?"

"Yes, sir."

"Then my son-in-law's postulation that Susan and Robbie were abducted is erroneous."

"Yes."

"Then how did Susan . . . ?" Bart didn't want to continue. He couldn't think these things. He didn't want to know these things. Wife beating was something that happened to backwater girls who had the misfortune to hook up with dull-witted bayou boys. Such things didn't happen to decent girls from good New Orleanian homes. Such things didn't happen to his daughter.

"Her husband beat her, Mr. Beaulieu. If she ran this time, it's my bet it's happened before. I don't know how many times . . ."

"Annette had heard some malicious gossip about Susan, but we talked about it. . . . We decided it wasn't true."

"It doesn't matter what you discussed, Mr. Beaulieu. Susan was beaten by her husband; I'll stake my job on it. I've seen this kind of thing a thousand times over the years. Girls from good homes, respectable families . . . girls from not-so-good homes. The stories are different, but the patterns are the same."

"Susan?" Bart Beaulieu was in shock.

"When did you hear these rumors, sir?"

"Susan . . ." Bart looked out over the meticulous gardens where red and yellow hibiscus and orange daylilies bloomed in profusion. "January."

As the lieutenant made notes, Bart Beaulieu's eyes traveled past the gardens to the tennis court where he'd taught Susan to play when she was eight years old.

"I'll never get the hang of this, Daddy," Susan said after missing her ninth serve. She was dressed in a white pleated

tennis skirt and a white blouse, and she wore her long blond hair in a thick braid down her back. She looked like Annette had at this age, Bart often remarked to friends; he and Annette had grown up together.

"We aren't going to quit until you return at least one of my serves. I won't have it be said that my daughter is a quitter."

"Oh, all right!"

The ball bounced into the front court on Susan's side. She swung at it with her forehand and sent it smashing over the net.

Susan's eyes were as big as saucers. "Did you see that, Daddy? I did it! I did it!"

Bart jumped over the net, picked up his daughter, and twirled her up and onto his shoulder. "I knew you could do it, Susan. You're my daughter!"

"That's right, Daddy." She leaned down and kissed the top of his head.

They marched to the porch, where Annette was watching them in the shade. Annette looked cool and elegant, as always. "It's very important for you to learn to play tennis well, dear," Annette said.

"Why is that, Mummy?"

"As you get older, you must fit in with all the other young people in our crowd, and everyone plays tennis and golf. And it's very important that you be accepted, dear. Very important, indeed."

"That's right. What you do and say; how you conduct yourself is a direct reflection upon us and the Beaulieu name. You must always remember my good reputation in this city and never do anything that would jeopardize my standing. You do understand, don't you, Susan?"

"I think so."

Annette touched her cheek. "You want Daddy and me to always be proud of you, don't you?"

"Yes, of course."

"Then you will always do the proper thing, won't you?"

"Oh, yes, Mummy. Yes."

Bart Beaulieu knew why Susan hadn't told them anything about her problems with Jim. He knew why she had disappeared from their lives without a note or call. He knew why they might never hear from their only child again, and he had no one to blame but himself.

"I . . . I didn't know . . ." Bart was saying as he looked back at the revealing spectres of the past on the tennis court.

Lieutenant Roberts nodded his head sadly. "I know, sir."

"I never liked Jim . . . from the very beginning. Actually, it was too late by the time she brought him home. She was already pregnant. She was only eighteen at the time, had only been in college two months. I guess she trusted him too much."

"That happens, sir."

Bart's eyes were cold, distant, and vengeful when he looked back at Lieutenant Roberts. "Not to *my* daughter it doesn't. Once maybe. But not twice."

"Mr. Beaulieu, we'll do everything we can to find your daughter."

Bart tried to control the rage he felt toward Jim Kidd, but the struggle was nearly too much for him. "Tell me, Lieutenant Roberts. If you find her, what will happen to her?"

"That's up to Susan. She can file for divorce. She could go back to him; that happens more than you'd want to know. They'll have to work out their differences—"

"The son of a bitch beat my daughter and you think I'm going to let her work out her differences?"

"You may not have much say in the matter, sir. It *is* Susan's life."

"Well, she's not doing very well with it, is she?"

Roberts dropped his head to his notepad and scribbled more

111

words onto the page. He closed the notepad and put it back into his shirt pocket. "I think she's doing the best she can right now, sir."

Angrily, Bart shoved his hands into his pockets.

"I have to be going, sir."

Bart didn't move. Roberts began walking back into the house to the hall and the front door. Suddenly Bart stirred and called after the officer. "Do me a favor, Lieutenant Roberts?"

"What's that?"

"Leave Susan be."

"I'd like to. Let's just pray she hasn't crossed the state line."

"Why's that?"

"We'd have to call in the feds, because then Susan would be guilty of kidnapping her own son. Mr. Kidd could have her put in prison. The feds don't let up, Mr. Beaulieu . . . ever." Roberts turned around and let himself out the front door, closing it quietly behind him.

Bart Beaulieu felt as if the earth had opened up and swallowed him. He sank back into his chair with a thud. "Susan . . . my baby. . . . This is all my fault. My fault . . ." Bart had never had an occasion in his life to cry, but today he did, and he didn't care who saw his tears.

Chapter Twelve

"This is the last time I can do this for you, Star," Sandra said as she handed Susan an envelope filled with two weeks' salary in cash.

"Am I fired?" Susan's voice was fearless, but her insides felt rocky.

Sandra's placid face ebbed into concern. "Aren't you happy here?"

"Yes. In fact, I find I'm enjoying myself more than I'd thought I would."

"Then there's no real problem. What I meant was that I can't pay you in cash anymore. You'll need to apply for a Texas state driver's license, and then next week I'll start taking out taxes and Social Security. You won't have as much take-home pay, of course, but the benefits will be better."

Susan stared at her employer. "You're not serious . . ."

"My accountant tells me this could be a potentially very serious situation. I hate doing this to you so soon, you trying to get on your feet and all, but it can't be helped."

Susan didn't want to be forced into any further explanations of any kind. "It's okay, really. I'll have all the proper identification on Monday. How would that be?"

Sandra was smiling more easily now. "Great. This helps me out a great deal." Sandra waited silently as two girls dressed in company uniforms came into the office, collected their paychecks, and left. "Look, Star, or whatever your real name is—"

"It really is Star."

"I know you're on the run from something or somebody and, frankly, I don't want to hear a single word of your story. What I also don't want is any kind of trouble with the federal government. My company is watched a bit more closely than would be normal for most because this is a maid service, and Mexican girls seem to pick this kind of work before they even cross the border. This city is a mecca for aliens. I screen my girls fairly well, and I can tell when they're lying to me. Just like I know that you're lying."

Susan began sputtering her protests to the contrary, but Sandra held up her hand to stop her. "Don't worry about it. It goes no further than here. I put the word out long ago that if a girl came to me, she had to be clean. At least she had to show me a green card and some ID. Then, if the feds have a problem, I'm out of the picture. Do you understand that?"

"Absolutely."

"Good." Sandra was smiling. "I'm sure it's just that you've been really busy since your arrival and with work and moving; you haven't had a chance to get to the license bureau."

"That's right. I've been very disorganized."

"Monday, then?" Sandra asked.

"Fine," Susan assured her cheerily.

"Good. See you then," Sandra said, dismissing Susan.

Susan walked toward the car where Micaela was sitting

with the air conditioner running while she filled out her bank deposit slip and endorsed her paycheck.

Susan swallowed hard, trying to remain calm at the thought of FBI men looking for her. She had wanted to protect herself and Robbie, not run them down danger's alley. However unwittingly, she had done just that. She had to protect Robbie at all costs. There was nothing she wouldn't do for him. Nothing.

Susan got into the car and Micaela smiled. "Mind if we stop at my bank?"

"Not at all. In fact, I think I'll see about getting an account myself."

"Okay," Micaela said.

Micaela drove to a bank near the apartments and parked the car, and the two women went through the glass doors to the busy lobby. While Micaela stood in line to deposit her paycheck, Susan inquired of one of the secretaries in the new accounts section what was required to open a checking account.

A green-eyed young woman dressed in a colorful print dress smiled at Susan as she answered, "The usual. Texas driver's license or some picture ID, Social Security Number, and a minimum of a two-hundred-dollar deposit. Would you care to open an account today?"

"Not today. I'm in a hurry, but I'll be back next week," Susan lied to the secretary.

Susan turned around and watched as Micaela walked away from the teller's window with her deposit slip.

It was such an ordinary procedure, Susan thought, depositing money in a bank account. A simple task she'd undertaken a thousand times in her life. And now, Susan thought, she'd never envied anyone as much as she did Micaela. Somehow, some way, she had to reinvent herself legally.

As they drove home, Susan glumly looked out the window at the stream of fast-food restaurants, clothing stores, bookstores, quick-stop markets, and print shops. Susan's head spun around as they stopped at a red light. Not ten yards behind them was a print shop with a huge sign in the window that read PASSPORT AND ID PHOTOS TAKEN HERE.

"Could we go around the corner and go back to that print shop over there?" Susan asked a bit anxiously.

"Sure. What do you need?" Micaela asked.

"I won't take but a few minutes." Susan was nearly sitting on the edge of her seat. This was her lucky day! And to think she'd nearly missed seeing that sign. She didn't need a driver's license; she just needed a photo ID. Why hadn't she thought of that before? As Micaela stopped the car, Susan quickly undid her seat belt and dashed out the door.

Inside the shop a dozen copiers, printing machines, and telephones created an ear-splitting cacophony. Had Robbie been with her, he would have thrown his hands over his ears, Susan thought. A young dark-haired man wearing an Astros baseball cap and NO FEAR T-shirt and jeans finished taking a telephone order.

"Howdy. What can I help you with today?"

"I'd like a photo ID."

"Sure." The young man took out his order pad and pulled a pencil from behind his ear. "Name and all the particulars first."

"Star Kaiser." Susan gave him her name, address, the telephone number to the complex, and her false Social Security Number.

"Could I see your card?"

"What card?"

"Social Security card. And I'll need your birth certificate, too."

Susan felt her stomach turn into knots and her face flush crimson. She smiled wanly and pretended to look in her purse. "Just a minute." She searched through cosmetics, gum wrappers, and her key to the apartment. "How silly of me." Her smile fell from her face.

The young man tapped the pencil on his pad impatiently.

"I must have left them in my other purse," she said apologetically.

"Sure." He stuck the pencil behind his ear.

"I'll just have to come back," she said, shrugging her shoulders.

"That's okay. Just remember we're closed Thursday."

Susan stared at him blankly.

"The Fourth of July?" He looked at her as if she were from outer space.

Susan had never felt more alien in her life. "Right. I'll remember that."

Idiot. Imbecile. How dumb could she be? Of course they would want a birth certificate. Susan got into the car.

"What's the matter with you?" Micaela asked as they pulled out of the parking lot.

"I wanted to get an ID card and I forgot my birth certificate is all."

"Forgot it or don't have one?"

Susan remained silent.

"Jesus! What did you think you were doing, buying an ID bracelet?"

"I guess," Susan said flatly, folding her arms defensively across her chest. "Look, I already feel stupid enough without your input."

"Sorry; I didn't mean it the way it sounded. I only wanted to help. Really." Micaela patted her arm lightly. "You're really in a bind, aren't you?"

"I didn't realize how much. Sandra told me I had to have a driver's license and my Social Security card by next payday."

"I thought I told you myself that all the girls have to be able to drive, in case somebody is out sick."

"You did. I guess I didn't want to hear it. But I'm hearing it now," Susan said.

They drove into the complex and parked the car. Just as Susan opened her car door, Micaela grabbed her arm and pulled her back in. "Look, I can't promise anything, but let me see what I can do about helping you out."

"How could you possibily help?"

"Trust me and don't say anything to anyone yet. Okay?"

"Okay." Susan shrugged her shoulders, not understanding Micaela in the least.

Susan went around to the meeting room, where she usually found Robbie watching the other children, but today he was nowhere in sight.

Panic riddled Susan like a barrage of bullets as she looked from child to child. Her eyes couldn't scan the room fast enough. Where was Robbie? Was he hurt? Had Jim found him and taken him away? Susan felt her blood turn icy cold. "Max . . . ?" Fear sucked the air out of her lungs as she barely breathed out his name.

Toni Camello blew a lock of hair off her sweaty forehead as she hoisted a screaming two-year-old into her arms. "Max isn't here, Star. He's with Andie, helping with the decorations for the party. He told me he had your approval."

"I almost forgot! He's been telling me about everything they were going to do," she replied, pretending her heart wasn't making that banging sound in her ears.

Toni sensed Susan's alarm. "It is all right, isn't it? If you had some objections, I wouldn't have let him go. I know how protective we have to be these days . . ."

Susan tried to smile to reassure a now very worried Toni, but it felt as if her lips were made of plaster. "It's okay. I just forgot is all."

Toni expelled a sigh of relief. "They should be back from shopping. If they weren't out by the pool, they must be in her office."

"I'll look for him there."

Susan walked away from the meeting room, realizing how much on edge she was. In the past Susan had never used a baby-sitter she hadn't known nearly all her life. She remembered going to Camilla Brighton's house when Robbie was four or five, and often he would be outside playing when he should be getting ready to leave; she'd never thought a thing about it. There had been times when her mother had picked up Robbie from his preschool without Susan's knowledge, claiming she'd left a message on the answering machine, or that she'd discussed the arrangement with Susan but she had forgotten. Susan had thought more of the fact that either her mother was getting senile or that she was as "zoned out," as Jim had often accused her of being, but she had never panicked as she had today when she hadn't seen Robbie in the room.

For the first time Susan became keenly aware of the razor's edge she was riding. For a brief period she had been lulled into a feeling of euphoria over the fact that she was free of Jim. The ultimatum from Sandra about the driver's license and then the incident at the print shop had put her life into sharp relief. Life outside her old milieu was teeming with pitfalls and dangers, and she couldn't help wondering if the family protection she'd always felt had been nothing more than an illusion.

Robbie's blond hair glistened in the July sun as he bent over a long row of clay pots. Each was filled nearly to the brim with sand, out of which stood three multicolored taper candles. Susan watched as Robbie went to a basket filled with such candles and carefully considered his color selections. Making certain he wasn't duplicating his colors, he would take three candles and then ram them as hard as he could into the sand. Susan thought it a wonder he didn't break the candles, but they were, mercifully, just fine.

"Max!" Susan waved as she approached.

He stood and yelled back, "Hi, Mom! Come look what I did for the party."

As Susan entered the pool area, she chided herself for her earlier misgivings. *He's okay. He's okay.* She felt herself become calm.

Robbie hugged her close when she bent down to him. When he kissed her cheek the inside of her mouth tingled, just the way it had when he'd been a baby and given her slobbery half licks and half kisses.

Robbie was immune to his mother's musings and quickly turned back to his handiwork. "I have to go back and pat the sand around each one, Andie said, to make sure they don't fall down." Robbie squatted next to the newest pot and tamped the sand with his little palm. He screwed his head half around on his shoulders in a way that only children seemed able to do, and said, "Do you think it's okay that I used all these pretty colors?"

"I think it's lovely. Why? Don't you like them?"

"The other kids said I had to do them in red, white, and blue."

"Oh." Susan smiled at his intense concern over the correctness of his task. "Did you ask Andie what her color scheme was going to be?"

"She already told me: red, white, and blue. But I thought that was kinda boring."

"Robb . . . Max. If the hostess has planned on a patriotic theme, don't you think you should do it her way?"

Robbie looked in the basket at the dearth of red, white, and blue candles that remained. "She gave me all these . . ." He looked down at the fuchsia, purple, and royal blue candles in his hand. "It would be a shame not to use them." He looked up at Susan with eyes needing to be filled with acceptance.

"I agree. Maybe I could work with you and Andie, and together we could blend everything together."

"That would be great, Mom!"

Just then Andie came down the winding pathway, her arms overloaded with flags; poles; red, white, and blue windsocks; plastic streamers, and cardboard cutouts of Uncle Sam and the Statue of Liberty. Andie took one look at the pots Robbie had finished and stopped dead in her tracks.

"I think this is going to be harder than we thought," Susan said to Robbie.

Robbie glanced down longingly at his handiwork and mentally said good-bye to his ideas.

Andie walked forward, never taking her eyes from the pots. She looked like a one-man Fourth of July parade to Robbie, laden down as she was.

"Let me help you," Susan offered and took the streamers and flags from Andie. When she did she realized that everything was sun-faded. Andie had used these decorations many, many times. These were Andie's familiar treasures, Susan thought. The last thing Susan had wanted was a confrontation over sentiment.

"I . . . I thought"—Andie looked at Susan and then to Robbie's anticipation-filled eyes—"that we were doing red, white, and blue."

Robbie didn't understand why his mother had shifted her sympathy to Andie, nor why Andie kept staring at his pots with confusion knitting her brow. If she didn't like them, why didn't she just say so? He would remake them for her, but first he would have his say. "I liked the happy colors better."

"Happy?" Andie blinked slowly.

"Yeah. I thought it was a party."

"It is." Andie put her aged decorations on one of the chaise longues. "I like it."

"What?"

"You do?" Robbie was surprised. He watched as a bright smile formed on Andie's face. "You do!"

Andie looked at Robbie. "The Fourth of July has always been my favorite holiday. Some people like Christmas or maybe Easter the best. For me it was the Fourth. Picnics, fireworks, barbeque, bands playing, parades, and lots of flags and balloons. What could be more festive? Every year I plan and put on this party for myself. I decorate the pool area and buy the watermelons, sparklers for the kids, and the ice cream for late at night when we can watch the stars here by the pool. Everybody in the complex has always chipped in, bringing all their grills, and we potluck everything. But I can tell by looking at my decorations here that I've let myself get stale. It's time we livened up the place. Try something different. Yes, that's the thing. This year we'll surprise everyone. What do you say?''

"All right!" Robbie shouted and high-fived Andie.

"We can still use the red-and-white-checked tablecloths. It doesn't cost anything to switch to multicolored balloons. And the fireworks are already multicolored. It'll look like a festival.''

"A happy festival," Andie said as she hugged Robbie by scrunching his shoulders together. "Thanks, Max, for helping me to change.''

Robbie smiled up at his new friend. "You're welcome.''

In all their different guises, holidays were always a time for reflection for Susan. As she sat by the pool watching Robbie swim laps that Fourth of July, she laid her head back and let the sun bathe her face. Someone's portable radio was turned up and the words to a sad song wafted across the pool and hit the chords of Susan's heart with stunning accuracy. She hadn't planned or wanted the tears that filled her eyes, and she especially hadn't asked for the memory that made her heart bleed.

Susan had brought her grandmother's wedding ring quilt for them to sit on while they waited and watched for the fireworks display over Lake Pontchartrain.

Jim had sprayed them both with insect repellent, opened

the small cooler, handed Susan a can of soda, and opened a beer for himself. Seldom in her life with Jim had he ever spoken of his own family, except to say that his parents were dead, but on that night he seemed to be caught between the moonlight and earth. He kept his focus on the heavens, ostensibly to catch the first of the fireworks, but now that Susan reflected upon it, she realized he was in a world of his own.

"I've never seen real fireworks," he said musingly.

"Aw, c'mon. Everybody has been to the fireworks," she teased, and punched his arm in a lighthearted manner.

"I haven't. I never did anything as a kid that most kids do. I always had to work."

Susan was intrigued. *"Doing what?"*

"Cows. I milked 'em, herded 'em, branded 'em, castrated 'em. I hated it. I can still smell their seared flesh and hear them groan and scream in that way only cattle can when someone has tortured them. I could never understand the purpose of it all."

"Your parents were ranchers?"

"Yes." Jim kept his eyes on the stars. *"I remember nights similar to this, only the stars are brighter in Wyoming. Maybe it's because there were no city lights to steal their glow. We used to sit around huge bonfires and watch the sky, and the air was so clean and crisp, you could crack it with your hand."*

"Sounds wonderful."

"I hated it."

Susan touched his neck. He flinched, as if she'd burned him. She immediately pulled her hand away, but he kept staring at the stars.

"Why did you hate it, Jim?"

"I hated being poor. I loved the land, though. I'd like to

go back someday, but not until I'm rich. Filthy, stinking rich. I want to own it all.''

''And if you did . . . own it all, I mean. What would it be like then?''

''It would make everything all right.''

Susan was too young at the time to travel into the inner labyrinths of Jim's world. She only knew that something back there in his past had hurt him, because she could feel his pain and hear it in his voice.

Gingerly, she touched the hair at his temple. This time he didn't flinch. ''I love you, Jim.''

''Do you really?'' His voice held surprise, even suspicion.

''Yes, I do. With all my heart.''

''I find that hard to believe.''

''But, Jim, we're married. Of course I love you. You love me, don't you?''

''As much as I'm able, darlin'. As much as I'm able.''

Suddenly he turned to her just as the first of a series of resplendent fireworks filled the sky with shimmering light. He grabbed her by the shoulders and pulled her to his chest. ''You do love me, don't you? Don't you? Promise me you'll never leave me. Promise me we'll be happy and always be together.''

''Of course I promise.''

He'd kissed her then, ravaging her lips with his, plunging his tongue into the interior of her mouth, claiming her as his possession, and she'd allowed him to do it. There was desperation in his kisses, and Susan had welcomed the excitement of it all.

Though she had already borne him a son, it was on that night that she had opened her heart to Jim and let him in.

Too easily, Susan remembered what it was like in those early days, to lie in Jim's arms, to have him love her. She remembered the excitement he brought to her life, the extravagant flowers on her birthday and dinner at an expensive restaurant when they could barely pay the telephone bill. She remembered that in his own way he'd made her breathe life into her lungs and experience emotions she'd never dreamed existed.

The song continued to play. Chills covered Susan's body, though she baked in the hot sun.

At that moment Susan wanted to hold Jim . . . just one more time, but only in the way that it had been in her memory. Susan had fallen in love with the hurt and frightened little boy who lived deep inside Jim. It was that boy she wanted to care for, guide, and help. It was he who pulled her back to Jim when she'd thought to leave him years ago. It was he who made her smile and who made her feel guilty. Tears streamed down her cheeks as she remembered the love she'd given Jim; a love she could never have with him again because he was no longer the same person.

The song ended and the deejay began advertising a special for a set of radial tires. Susan instantly sat up, wiped her tears with the palm of her hand, and looked across the pool for Robbie. She waved to him and he waved back.

This is how it happens, she thought to herself. It's been nearly a month since I left. Time enough to dispel the anxiety over running away. Time enough to miss someone . . . or the way they used to be. These feelings . . . they're the culprits that make women go back to the men who abuse them.

Chapter Thirteen

Angels roamed the netherworld, Susan knew, and that was why she paid no attention to the voice that said, "I want to help you."

It's just a dream, she told herself.

But the voice persisted, and as it did it took on the character of Micaela's voice.

"Star, I want to help you." Micaela finally nudged Susan's arm as she slept by the pool.

Susan opened her eyes and glanced around her to get her bearings. Not a minute ago she would have vowed she had been with Jim. "Sorry; I guess I fell asleep."

"Andie said she'd keep an eye on Max for you while we go up to my apartment."

Susan looked to the pool and found no sign of Robbie. Still a bit disoriented, she quickly sat up, and then she saw Robbie with Andie, both loading ears of corn onto the grill of a huge oil-drum cooker. She looked back to Micaela.

"Help me with what?"

126

"Shhh!" Micaela replied and motioned for Susan to follow her.

Susan rose and waved to Robbie, but he was busily chatting with Andie and didn't notice his mother's departure.

He was probably telling her just how to roast the corn. Presoak in sugared ice water for an hour before roasting. Place on medium-heated coals. A quarter turn every fifteen minutes, Susan could almost hear him saying.

Susan caught up with Micaela on the winding path that led to the staircase to Micaela's apartment. "Why are you being so mysterious?" Susan asked bluntly.

Micaela inserted her key in the door and looked at Susan, giving her a quick shake of her head. "Come in."

Susan entered the apartment and Micaela quickly shut the door behind them.

"Luis thinks he can help you get your driver's license."

Susan laughed lightly. "How on earth could Luis do that?"

Micaela pulled up her shoulders and looked at Susan as if she were the dumbest woman on earth. "Luis does this for a living."

Susan stared at Micaela blankly for a full half minute. "Ooooh myyy God!" Susan's hands flew to her cheeks and her eyes opened round and wide in surprise. "He's a forger?"

It was Micaela's turn to laugh. "An angel of mercy to those who need him."

Susan instantly untied her bundle of previously set convictions, resorted them according to her new situation, and realized that Micaela spoke the truth. "He is an angel! And so are you!" Susan threw her arms around Micaela. "I never thought I would break the law so willingly."

"As they say, 'A time and a place for everything.' "

Just then Luis walked out of the "office" bedroom. Smiling, he shook Susan's hand. "How you doin'?"

"Fine," she replied hesitantly. Suddenly the import of Luis's occupation hit her full force. "Thank you for helping me, Luis . . . but do you mind me asking . . . isn't this dangerous for you?''

"*Sí*. It can be. So far I have been able to outthink de police.'' He tapped his temple with his forefinger and winked at her. "However, I think that de people from Mexico need me very much. You are my first gringa.''

They all laughed, and then Luis ushered Susan into his office.

Susan was stunned at the computers, file cabinets, Fax machine, laminating machine, cutters, and racks of forms that met her eyes. "It takes all this?''

"*Sí* and very much more.''

"But it all fits in the van when we feel we need to move on,'' Micaela said. "Well, I guess I'll start my salsa for the barbeque tonight while you two get to work.'' Micaela shut the door and left Susan with Luis.

Luis sat down on a swivel stool that was perched atop a slick sheet of plastic that enabled him to roll from computer to file cabinet and then over to the laminating machine.

He turned on the computer and pulled up a list of names on the screen. "I have to give you a new name.''

"I can't use Star Kaiser anymore?''

Luis's face scrunched into an uncertain grimace. "It be preety hard. But we check it out.'' He scrolled down the screen and as he did, Susan realized that he was scanning a list of obituaries. These were all dead people's names, and their respective Social Security Numbers. "It must have taken you a long time to compile this list.''

"Naa. I been stealin' them for a long time.''

"How?'' Susan asked.

"First I take de names from de newspaper. Den I get numbers from de state office. Sometimes from de driver's license bureau or de marriage bureau or hall of records. Depends. Each county is different.''

"How do you get the Social Security Numbers?''

"Dat's what I been tellin' you. I use de computer. See? Watch. I show you."

Luis pressed some buttons on his keyboard. "Where you born?"

"In . . . in New Orleans." Susan was uncertain whether she should tell him the truth, but she decided Luis was in more trouble with the law than she would ever be.

Luis's fingers flew across his keyboard. "Name?"

"Susan Beaulieu," she replied, and then spelled it out for him. "Daughter of Bart and Annette, if that helps."

"Sí." Luis continued punching keys.

Suddenly, before her eyes, Susan saw her name, her birth certificate number, her Social Security Number, all the information regarding her marital status and date of marriage, and then the screen scrolled down further and she saw information about Robbie and his birth appear.

"God, that's frightening!"

"Sí. I know! But wonderful. No?"

"That's my whole life . . . reduced to numbers and dates, and what's worse, they're available to anyone."

"No! That not true! Not anyone. Only to smart people like Luis. I am de best at my job! It take me years . . . years to learn all dis computer crap," Luis replied indignantly.

"I'm sorry, Luis. I didn't mean it to sound the way it did. It's just a shock, that's all."

"Sure. Sure." Luis banged away on the keys. "Now. We gotta give you a new name."

"I'd like to keep this one. I'm kind of getting used to it now and I like it."

Luis shook his head so hard that the crucifix and St. Christopher medal that hung around his neck clanged together. "Weemen."

Susan indulged his petulance, but she stood firm on her idea.

"Dere is no *Kaiser* I can use. Eet can be much easier if

you change your name now. See? Very simple. We take de name of this dead person, I put it on one of dees forms,'' Luis rolled the stool over to his filing cabinet and withdrew a Texas State driver's license application that looked to Susan like the real thing. "I retype dis information on de form. Laminate. And done." He expelled a huge sigh of exasperation. "But no. You gotta have dis name you like. So, here's what we gonna do."

Luis rolled over to another filing cabinet and withdrew a marriage certificate form. He pulled out a caligraphy pen, filled it with black ink, and set it down. Then out of a second drawer in the filing cabinet he retrieved an original marriage certificate. "What day you like?"

"Day?"

"To get married on. How many days you been married to . . ." Luis thought for a moment. "Bob Kaiser. Dat okay?"

"Okay."

Luis held up a warning finger. "Can't be more dan sixty days in Texas. You gotta get your name changed on de license in sixty days."

"Okay. June seventh, 1996." Susan used the day she'd left Jim as her wedding date.

Luis carefully wrote down the date. "Star what?"

"Huh?"

"Last name . . . before you marry Bob."

"Sloan."

Luis grimaced as he wrote it down. "I like Kaiser better, too." Luis finished filling out the bogus marriage certificate and then handed it to Susan.

"Okay. On Tuesday you take dis to the license bureau. You tell them you wanna get your license transferred to Texas. You tell dem you got new address and new name."

"But I don't have an old license."

"Ah!" His eyes twinkled merrily as he spun his stool around and zipped first to the file cabinet to withdraw a form.

Quickly, he went back to the computer, scrolled a sea of Social Security Numbers in front of him and wrote one of them down. Then he went to the typewriter and rolled the form into it. He hit the keys with lightning speed and the accuracy of one who knows what he is doing. He rolled the finished form off the carriage and then scooted the stool to the far right side of the room, where a huge camera sat on a tripod.

"Stand over there on de mark." He pointed to a white piece of tape on the carpet.

Susan did as she was instructed, thinking how similar this procedure was to the real thing.

Luis looked through the eye of the camera. Then he looked up at Susan. "Part your hair down de middle."

"Why?"

"So you look younger. Dis has to look like old license."

Susan used her fingers to part her hair. She smiled.

"Don't smile!" Luis commanded as he shot the picture.

Luis pulled out the film and left the room. "Be right back," he said and crossed the hall to the bathroom.

When he entered the office again after fifteen minutes he had a finished passport-type photograph in his hand. He trimmed the edges of the photo with a pair of scissors and carefully pasted it to the phony driver's license form. Then he rolled his stool over to the laminating machine and laminated the license.

He took the license and with a razor peeled two of the edges of the lamination back. Then he took the license and jammed it into the dirt of a potted fern that sat next to his computer. He banged the card on the desk several times and made some scratches in the laminate with a steel brush. He handed it to Susan.

"It looks real! Definitely used-looking, as it should be."

"I do good work," Luis said proudly, crossing his arms over his chest.

"You certainly do."

"Now, take it to the bureau. They will take de old card, give you a new temporary license once they see the marriage certificate. You don't need proof of address. Jus' tell 'em. Make sure you go at eleven-thirty. Noon is too late. Everybody tinks dey go at eleven to avoid de rush and that ees de rush. Then all the peoples are super busy. Dey jus' want to get through with de work. Dey don' look so close. Okay?"

"This will work?"

"Sure ting."

"I can't thank you enough, Luis. How much do I owe you for all this?"

"Micaela took care of eet." He smiled broadly at her.

"She shouldn't have done that."

Luis opened the door for Susan. "Eet is my pleasure, believe me."

Luis remained in the office while Susan went to the kitchen to visit with Micaela.

Micaela was still chopping fresh tomatoes. "He got you all fixed up?"

"Yes, and I can't thank you enough. Micaela, he told me that you're paying for this. I can't let you do that. I'll repay you."

Micaela's smile was just as enigmatic as Luis's had been. She waved Susan's protests away as she went to the refrigerator and pulled out a plastic bag filled with fresh jalepeños. "Keep your money. You'll need it. Besides, you can't pay this debt."

"Why not?"

"I told Luis . . ." Micaela started to laugh as she pulled Susan over and leaned close to her ear. "I told Luis I would . . ." She finished with a whisper in Susan's ear and laughed uproariously.

After Susan replaced her gaping jaw she started laughing along with Micaela.

*   *   *

132

The next morning Susan arranged with Sandra to take an hour off from their first assignment in order to go to the motor vehicle bureau to get her Texas driver's license.

She arrived at eleven-thirty, just as Luis had told her, and sure enough the place was swamped. She took her number and waited over half an hour to get to the counter, but when she did the clerk shoved a "change of name" form at her and had her sign it. Susan surrendered her old license, told them her new address, and agreed to be a total organ donor, which was indicated on the back of her temporary card. She passed the vision test, had her picture taken, paid her sixteen dollars in cash, and was handed her temporary driver's license. The clerk told her to expect her new license in the mail within six weeks.

Susan walked out of the bureau looking at her new license. She was filled with the oddest sensation that today she truly was a new person. She was legally Star Kaiser of Houston, Texas. It was a good feeling.

Chapter Fourteen

New Orleans

Jim Kidd awoke in a profuse sweat, screaming Susan's name. He bolted to an upright position and immediately reached for his wife, but she wasn't there. He patted and then began slapping the empty bed next to him. He fell onto her side of the bed, and with his fist he banged at the down-filled pillow. "Susan! Susan! Why aren't you here when I need you?" Jim cried.

He cried until his sobs settled so deeply in his chest, he was afraid they would become trapped and never escape him. He didn't like being this afraid. He was more than afraid; he was terrified. Susan was gone and she was the only one who could save him. She had always saved him in the past from his nightmares. What had happened that she wasn't there for him now? How could his world change so swiftly, and with such vast-reaching effects, simply because Susan had left?

How had he come to depend on her so much? How had he come to need her?

Jim wiped his hand over his perspiring face. He pushed back his tears and opened his eyes. As they accustomed themselves to the faint night shadows, he remembered that he'd had nightmares as a child. Neither his mother nor his father ever came to his rescue. In fact, they had scolded him all the more for disturbing their sleep. Most of the time he never told them about his nightmares; he kept the workings of his dream life to himself. He didn't want anyone—not his family, the neighborhood kids, or his friends at school—to think he was a sissy. He didn't dare tell anyone he was afraid of the dark; afraid of the life his mind conjured up during sleep.

Instead Jim stayed awake. He read. He worked connect-the-dots and crossword puzzles. He put model airplanes together beneath his Flintstones-imprinted sheets and bedspread using a flashlight to see his work. Jim was proud of the nocturnal world he kept secret from his parents.

Jim got out of bed and went to the bathroom to splash cold water on his face. *Jesus. I haven't thought of those days for years. I'd forgotten all that.*

Jim didn't like to think of himself as a child. In his mind he was an adult—a functioning, productive member of society who played by the rules others made so that he could make it to the top. Life was serious business to Jim. He didn't like to play with anyone or at anything. He played golf and tennis solely for the business contacts he could make on the courts or fairways.

Jim wiped off his face with a towel. "That's why I don't like Robbie," he said aloud without thinking as he walked back into the bedroom and sat on the edge of the bed. *Children . . . toys . . . playtime. I hated all that stuff as a kid. I hate it even more now. Robbie has it too easy. Susan always did baby him too much.*

Jim couldn't tell if the smell of Opium came from his

mind's eye or if Susan had just entered the room. "Susan?" He thought he could nearly see the outline of her form among the night shadows that played on the wall.

The drapes were drawn back, leaving only the lace panels covering the window. Moonlight cast a flowered pattern across the floor. Suddenly Jim remembered that Annette and Susan had sewn those lace panels together by hand. At the time Susan had been so proud of her creation, and Jim could have cared less. He was busy.

"But, honey, don't you think they're lovely?" Susan had asked him from atop a stepladder as she finger-pleated the last fold.

"Sure, sure," he said, not even looking at his wife. He tossed his briefcase on the bed and then immediately went to the closet and routed through his built-in shelves for a sheaf of vitally important papers.

"But Jim, I've worked on them all week. Couldn't you at least *look* at them?"

"Eureka!"

Jim emerged from the closet with a portfolio, which he held triumphantly over his head.

"Now *this* is important!" He tossed the papers in his briefcase and closed it, barely noticing his wife's crestfallen face. "I'm off." Jim raced out the door.

On his way down the hall he passed Robbie, who was licking a frozen pushup Popsicle. "Daddy!" Robbie started to throw his sticky hands around Jim's pantleg.

"Get away from me!" Jim sidestepped his two-year-old son and darted down the hall. "I'll be late!" he yelled and was gone.

The scent of Susan's perfume continued to hang in the air, but Jim realized this, too, was just his imagination.

Jim sat on the edge of the bed, wondering why these visions of the past were coming back to him. Why hadn't he commented on Susan's work when she'd so obviously needed his approval? Why had he never really looked at these damn curtains until tonight? He rose and went to the window. He touched the fabric. There was something familiar about the curtains.

Suddenly he dropped the edge of the curtain and jumped back from the window as if he'd been burned.

"I hate those curtains! I hate them! I hate them!"

Then, suddenly, the dream he'd been dreaming that night came back to him. The nightmare he'd been pushing down into his subconscious came thundering through a dark tunnel of awareness and into the light.

My mother had curtains like this. . . . He started to reach out to the window again but snatched his hand back. He was shaking and sweating profusely. Suddenly, as if time and space had altered themselves, Jim's bedroom was transformed to the old farmhouse he'd lived in when he was only five.

"Mommy! No!" Jim screamed at the top of his lungs as he raced through the kitchen toward the parlor.

"Come back here, you little bastard!" Olga Kidd, a huge, mannish-looking woman, overtook her tiny son in three large steps. With arms the size of hams and thighs twice as large, she scooped Jim up by the nape of his neck. "Don't you ever, ever come into my kitchen tracking dirt in like that. You and that goddamn fool dog of yours are going to get it. I told you and told you . . ." Olga started swinging her hand to swat Jim on his buttocks.

Jim began twisting and struggling to free himself. "No! No! Don't hurt me!"

"I'll hurt you all I want. I'm your mother!"

As Jim twisted free from his mother's clutches, Olga quickly turned to the top of the battered china cabinet, which held little of value these days. Most of the pretty blue-flowered

*china was either chipped or at the bottom of a rusted trash
barrel, broken over the head of her often drunken husband.
Her fat, square-shaped fingers seized a long, thin switch.*

*Jim raced as far as the windows in the living room before
the end of the switch caught him around his legs. He fell into
the lace curtains and clutched at them as he screamed in pain
at the first lashing.*

*"Mommy! No! Stop!" Jim clung to the curtains, pressing
his face into the white flowered pattern. The second switching
drew blood. The third laced the top of his fleshy thighs with
a cross pattern. Blood trickled down his leg.*

*"Maybe that will break your spirit!" Olga said as she
placed the switch back on top of the china cabinet and left
the room, fully satisfied that Jim had paid for his crime of
dirtying her floor.*

Jim had cried. His eyes were so filled with tears, he could
barely see the curtains anymore. His nose ran. He cried some
more. He wanted to hurt his mother for what she had done
to him, but she was bigger than he was. He could do nothing
about his situation because he was a still a kid.

Jim realized that day that the worst thing in the world was
to be a kid. Kids had no power. They had no strength. He
couldn't fight back because the whole world was bigger than
he was. He couldn't run away because he had no place to go.
He wasn't old enough to have a job so he could get money
to pay for a train ticket, the way he'd seen his Uncle Lester
do when he came to visit from Oregon.

From Jim's experience, being a kid meant he had to do
chores at four in the morning, helping to milk the cows. He
had to clean out the stables in the afternoons while his father,
Caleb, sat on the front porch in the shade talking to other
farmers. Jim wondered what all there was to talk about. Jim
was ordered about by both his mother and his father, and,
depending upon their mood, he was beaten, whipped,

switched, or slapped nearly every week of his life until he was eight.

At the age of eight Jim learned how to play their game. He knew to beware of the twitch in Olga's face when she was angry at Caleb; at those times he stayed as far away from the house as possible. When Olga was angry she would vent upon anyone within striking distance. Her rows with Caleb were notorious throughout the county. Olga never covered her black eyes and bruises, but rather wore them like honorariums for all to see. To Olga, attention of any kind, even if it was abuse, was a sign that her husband loved her.

At the same time, during Jim's life, he began doing odd jobs around their little town of Four Corners for whomever would hire a little kid. His pay was usually next to nothing, but he saved all the money, never telling his parents what he was doing or that he was paid. It wasn't until he was ten that his mother discovered at the Methodist Church Memorial Day social that Jim had been working as a stockboy for the local A & P grocery store.

Olga was in a rage when she confronted Jim with the truth. She started to go for her switch, but this time Jim was ready for her. He'd learned a lot in the past five years. He'd learned how to come and go in his own house with no one knowing. He'd learned that both his parents were alcoholics and that their actions weren't only predictable, but more easily circumvented than he thought. He'd learned that he had inherited some of his mother's genes; he was the largest boy in his class. Thus, at the age of ten, Jim was the size of most fourteen-year-olds.

Jim knew that he was fast on his feet due to a gym instructor at school whose personal preference for track-and-field events had forced Jim to run hurdles and the hundred-yard dash. The year before, his parents had paid little attention to the fact that Jim had come in first in every intramural race.

*   *   *

Jim bounded across the room, jumped to the top of the china cabinet as if he'd just gone for a basketball layup, grabbed the switch out of his mother's reach, and quickly raised his leg and broke the switch into four small pieces over his knee.

"Here!" he said triumphantly.

Olga's mouth dropped wide open. "What the hell you doin', boy?"

"You will never touch me again."

"The hell I won't! I'll do any goddamn thing I want. You're my kid and it's my duty to teach you right from wrong."

Jim's eyes were blazing with anger and long-suffered pain. "I'll walk out of here and you'll never see me again."

Olga pushed her fat arms at the air in front of her. "Aw, shut up! You ain't goin' nowhere. You're a kid. And you'll do as I say."

Jim shook his head. "You lay one finger on my body and I'll tell the counselor at school what's been going on here all these years. They put kids like me into foster homes."

"Go to hell."

Jim's upper lip curled as he spoke. "You won't have anyone to do your dirty work anymore if I'm gone."

Jim didn't wait for an answer but left the house immediately, hopping on his bike and riding down the dirt drive to the main road and then the four miles into town to the A & P. It was the first time in his life that Jim felt in control. He vowed that day that he would always remain in control. Always.

When Jim was thirteen years old he left home for good, and he never looked back. He went to Des Moines, where he easily passed for sixteen. He worked three jobs to pay for a bedroom in an old Victorian house that had been converted to apartments for Drake University students. He hung out with college guys who bought him all the beer he could drink and told him of their dreams of becoming accountants, lawyers, investment bankers, and doctors. He learned to dream their dreams and set goals for himself.

He got a GED, bought a car, and lost his virginity all in the same day when he was eighteen. Jim moved to New Orleans when all his ''friends'' graduated from college. He never told anyone about his past, and in time he'd learned precisely how to repress every incident that had happened to him before he moved to New Orleans. Once in New Orleans he got a job as a waiter in an oyster bar and began night school. He applied for grants and loans and finally attended Tulane full-time.

Since he was thirteen years old Jim had been telling the lie that his parents were dead so many times that it became his truth. He worked night and day at whatever project was facing him. He told himself that he had too much to do, that his work was too important for him to waste time sleeping.

Jim could never remember his nightmares, only that he awoke from them in a terrified sweat. Susan knew. She had held him and rocked him and told him that she loved him. She never knew why he cried out in the night, and she loved him enough never to ask. Jim hated himself for his weakness. He couldn't allow himself to be vulnerable, because if he did, he would lose control. Losing control was an intolerable situation to Jim. Sometimes Jim hated Susan for knowing about his nightmares. Other times he thought he wouldn't be able to live the night through if Susan wasn't there to show him she cared. Jim wanted Susan with him now, to help ease the pain, but she had vanished.

Jim told himself that he would learn how to cope with the nights without Susan. He had lived for years without her. He had taught himself how to survive on only a few hours sleep. The only problem with being a night person was that with the night came the booze.

Jim had no idea his consumption of alcohol had reached dangerous levels. Just as he'd created his own denial system about his past, he denied his present. He told Susan that she was "overreacting" when she complained that he drank too much. He didn't remember hitting her the first time, but he'd seen the evidence the next day. He made many excuses for himself, and most of them worked. Jim became incredibly successful at turning away from the truth.

However, after all these years Jim's truth was emerging like a sea serpent rising slowly from the depths of the abyss. Now he remembered his nightmare. Both his mind and his body recalled every detail of the day when he'd been sprawled against the white curtains like a criminal tied to a whipping post. It wasn't just a dream. It was real. It was his past. It was his childhood. He had lived it, and now through his dreams and memory he was being forced to live it again and again.

It was the worst of all possible hells, because his anguish was within him, and Jim was ill-equipped to deal with his demons.

Jim's body trembled as he clutched the lace curtains in his bedroom and pressed his face into the fabric. Suddenly he was that little boy again, being switched, bleeding onto the pretty white lace. He was filled with rage at what had been done to him. He was shaking at the enormity of his hatred ... at the ferocity that filled him ... wanting to kill his mother. He clutched the curtains and pulled, and with the full force of his strength he ripped them out of the wall, rod, brackets, and all.

"Ahhhhhhhh! I hate you! I hate you! I hate you...." Jim saw the vision of his mother and Susan blend into one malefic monster. He couldn't discern one from the other and projected his anger against his mother onto Susan.

He was powerless. Impotent. He was out of control, and

he hadn't the slightest idea how to right his world again . . . except to find Susan.

Jim fell to the floor amid the rubble he had created and cried the tears of a brokenhearted child.

Chapter Fifteen

"I could have your badge for this." Captain Michaud stubbed out a cheap cigar into a tin ashtray. He didn't put his hand over his mouth when he started a deep lung-throttling cough.

"You've said that before," Lieutenant Roberts replied quietly.

"This time I mean it. First you withhold evidence. Then you withhold information from the family, so that I got them breathing down my neck, too," Captain Michaud growled at his longtime co-worker and friend. "Jesus, Nate. Do you always have to do everything the wrong way?"

"I'm not wrong, here, Jess. The rule book is a joke. That's what's wrong."

"Aw, Jesus. Are we gonna start that crap again?" Captain Jess Michaud waved both hands dismissively at Lieutenant Roberts.

"You know damn well that if I call Mr. Kidd and tell him everything I've found out about his wife, he's gonna go after her and drag her back home. Then the next goddamn phone call I get is one sayin' Susan, there, is in the hospital with her face smashed to smithereens, that the kid o' hers is apoplectic, and the family gives me some cockamamy story that she fell down the stairs. Or worse, we get a child abuse case and somebody dies. . . . It makes the papers and you come back and tell me . . . *me,* mind you, 'cause it won't be you who takes the rap . . . that I screwed up.'' Roberts started pacing. ''Now, how many times we gotta run through this thing before somebody around here gets the damn picture, Jess? Huh?''

''Okay.'' Captain Michaud coughed hard, grabbed his handkerchief from his back hip pocket, and spit into it before returning it to his pocket.

''Why don't you give up those damn things? They're gonna kill you.''

''Shut up. Look who's talking anyway.'' Captain Michaud grabbed another cigar, tore off the band, looked at it, and then gently laid it back down on the desk. He stared at the cigar, wishing he had the guts to quit cold turkey. He started to pick up his matches but resisted the temptation.

Roberts looked away to the window while his superior composed himself.

''I know what you're saying, Nate. But the law is the law. You have to tell her husband what you've found out when he calls you.''

''That's just the point. Mr. James Kidd has not called. Her father . . . well, that's another story. Half my messages are from him. I told him what I thought he should know.''

''Which is?''

''That we're working on it. That we haven't found her and that I do think she's alive.''

Captain Michaud looked at the mountain of files on his desk. ''Shit. They all have a story, don't they?''

''Yep. They do.'' Roberts watched as a blue jay settled into a magnolia tree just outside the window. ''Some stories are so gruesome they make you sick to your stomach.''

Jess Michaud regarded his friend with a critical eye. ''Is that what's going on here?''

Nathanial Roberts looked back at his superior. ''Nope. This one breaks my heart.''

''That's worse.''

''I know.'' Nate raised his chin and took a deep breath. ''So, am I getting canned or what?''

Captain Michaud shook his head and smiled at his friend. ''You've been warned. Take my advice and don't get messed up in somebody else's domestic shit.''

Roberts smiled politely and then placed both his hands on top of the piles of papers on Captain Michaud's desk. He leaned close to Jess's face. ''Do you know why these piles on your desk are so high, Jess? Do you know why we've got a rape every four minutes in this town? Drugs? Drive-by shootings, gangs, murder . . . all this shit that keeps us pulling our hair out night and day? Because twenty, thirty, forty— hell, a hundred years ago, some cop like you told another cop not to get messed up in somebody else's domestic problems. That's why.

''I'm past my time here, Jess. I don't care much about what happens to me anymore, but I do care about that young woman out there and her little boy. If you want somebody to play by the rules on this one, go ahead. But by God, if you keep me on this case, I'm doin' it my way. I don't want to change the whole world, Jess. I just want to make one life a little bit better because I was there.''

Lieutenant Roberts stood up straight. ''What's it gonna be?''

Captain Michaud laughed and leaned back in his chair. ''Know what your real problem is, Nate?''

''No, what?''

''You don't think big enough. I *do* want to change the world.'' Captain Michaud picked up his cigar, looked at it, and tossed it into the trash can. "Get out of here."

Roberts didn't waste a second as he closed the office door behind him.

It wasn't until the fourth ring that Lieutenant Roberts picked up his telephone.

"Roberts here."

"Oh, thank goodness you're there, Lieutenant Roberts," Annette Beaulieu said with a great deal of trepidation in her voice. "I've never phoned a police station before and it was quite an experience just getting through to you. I think I've spoken to nearly everyone in your office."

"Precinct."

"Yes, well, I'm not all that familiar with the correctness of my terminology . . ."

"What can I do for you, Mrs. Beaulieu?"

"Well, I understand that my husband has been conducting most of the correspondence between you and us, and I, er, I was hoping that perhaps there was something you could tell me about . . . Susan."

He could hear Annette Beaulieu's heart leap to her throat at the mention of her daughter's name. He knew she was near the breaking point and he wished to hell there was something he could do about it.

This is the most ghastly part of my job, he thought to himself. The movies always made it look as if bullet-riddled bodies or a maimed robbery victim were the hardest things to deal with in police work, but that wasn't true. Telling a heart-sick parent that all his computers, all the state troopers, cops on the beat, and investigators in the State of Louisiana could not find her daughter and grandson; that was the most difficult thing he had to do.

Limbo was torturous geography, but that was exactly where Nate Roberts was directing Annette Beaulieu. "I have nothing more than what I've already told your husband, Mrs.

Beaulieu. Susan and Robbie were spotted taking a bus out of Alexandria to Little Rock. We've just gotten in the affidavits from both car dealers, the one where she sold the Taurus in Baton Rouge and now the one in Alexandria. And as I stated to your husband, when she was in Alexandria she purchased a bus ticket to St. Louis.''

"Do you think Susan would go to St. Louis?''

"You tell me. Does she know anyone there?''

"Yes. An old college friend, Jamie Wilkins. Bart and I have already called her, but she's heard nothing. We went through Susan's old yearbooks just as you asked.''

"Did you think of anyone that she might contact?''

"Not really, but we did make a few calls.''

"Any luck?''

Annette's deep breath was audible over the phone. ''No.''

Lieutenant Roberts could tell Annette was fighting the tears. ''I'm . . . we're doing all we can, Mrs. Beaulieu.''

Annette's voice finally cracked. Lieutenant Roberts felt as if he could hear each tear as it fell. ''Well, it isn't enough, Lieutenant, if you don't mind my saying so. I want to know that my daughter is safe. I . . . I don't know if she's dead or alive. . . . I don't know where she is. . . . I don't know if I'll ever see my grandson again. Please . . . you've just got to help us. You've just got to. I don't know who else to turn to. . . .''

Annette didn't wait for an answer and, uncharacteristically for a genteel lady, she hung up the phone without speaking her cordialities.

Just as Lieutenant Roberts hung up the receiver, Maisy O'Brien, former topless dancer turned excellent policewoman, stood in front of his desk and tossed down a long white envelope.

Nobody on the force really knew Maisy O'Brien's real name, since she'd used about a half dozen aliases in her ''show days,'' but they did all know that they could count on her. Now forty-nine years old, she looked half that. She had saved her money wisely and invested well during her years as a stripper so that she had enough money to buy the best plastic surgeons, the finest and most effective masseuses and facialists, and she took vacations when she felt she needed them. Maisy had a body that put Marilyn Monroe's curves to shame. She still boasted a twenty-three-inch waist, which she kept tightly cinched with her shiny black leather gun and holster belt. She kept her badge and silver buttons sparkling like rhinestones and her blue slacks tapered just a smidge too tight over her derriere.

In Maisy's opinion the only quirk to her personality was that she liked policework. When she quit show business and went back to school she found she had a gift for counseling work. Maisy knew her limitations better than anyone else, but unlike other people, she admitted to herself what those limitations were. Maisy didn't see herself hanging up a psychologist's shingle and counseling bored, middle-class housewives.

She liked throwing herself in the middle of "domestic altercations," and from her own experiences she knew that she wanted to be on the receiving end of 911 calls.

Lieutenant Roberts looked at the envelope and then up at Maisy. He smiled slowly. "Maze, is it sexual harassment to say that you give a whole new shape to the police uniform?"

"Are you trying to say that I look lovely today, Lieutenant?" she teased him back.

"I guess so."

She pointed to the envelope. "You owe me an oyster dinner at Felix's."

Roberts's eyes rounded in surprise. "You got the tickets?"

"Yes, sir. You land in Little Rock at three." Maisy looked at her watch. "You need to leave for the airport in fifteen minutes."

He picked up the envelope and shoved it into his shirt pocket. "I won't tell a soul."

"You better not." She perched her hand on her well-rounded hip. "The other guys will think I'm playing favorites."

He smiled back. "Well, are you?"

She winked at him. "You bet I am." She turned slightly, allowing him a breathtaking view of the contour of her breasts. Then she walked away.

"Damn. That woman almost makes me feel young again."

Roberts quickly gathered his things from his desk and made a phone call to Little Rock to confirm his appointment. When he left the precinct he didn't tell Captain Michaud where he was going, or why.

Little Rock, Arkansas

Lieutenant Roberts took a cab to the Greyhound bus terminal. When he walked inside the building he was met immediately by Raymond Gorman, the bus driver who had reported to the New Orleans police department's routine inquiries that he had picked up a young woman matching Susan Kidd's description.

Raymond Gorman was about forty-five years old, just over six feet tall, with hair as red as Arkansas clay. He had sky blue eyes rimmed with nearly invisible blond lashes and topped with thin, transparent-looking eyebrows that made his face look as if all his facial hair had been seared off in a fire. He had a mouthful of overly large, crooked teeth barely held back by a thin pair of lips. He wore what should have been a snappy uniform, clean and well pressed, but the fabric and buttons struggled so mightily to cover Raymond's enormously protruding stomach that he looked unkempt. Just the sight of Raymond made Lieutenant Roberts check his own shirt to make certain it was neatly tucked into his waistband.

"Howdy do, Lieutenant." Raymond pumped Roberts's

arm so hard, he thought the bus driver would tear his rotator cuff.

"Fine. Fine." Roberts broke away. "Got quite a grip there."

"Nature of the job," Raymond yucked with a hayseed accent. He shoved up his shirtsleeve and flexed his biceps. "It takes a lot of muscle to make them turns. I did a three-sixty in the parking lot just a week ago."

Lieutenant Roberts hoped his gaping mouth wasn't too obvious. "Amazing."

"I 'spose you want to go someplace private to talk."

"That would be good." Roberts nodded.

Raymond held out his arm. "I took care of it, 'fore you got here. I told Hattie to stay out of the office while we took care of bidness."

"Fine." Roberts followed Raymond into a cubicle of a room that was stacked in one corner with old crates of small Coke bottles. There were two plastic and metal chairs, one harvest gold and the other avocado green. Roberts wondered if they were corporate colors. The flourescent light overhead buzzed menacingly due to what looked like poor wiring.

"Have a seat," Raymond said.

Roberts chose the gold chair. He took out his notepad and pen.

Raymond sprawled in the chair opposite Roberts and crossed his huge arms over his enormous belly. Roberts realized that Raymond wasn't trying to act slovenly; it was simply that he was too long and too obese for the small chair. Thus, Raymond's legs were forced to shoot out in front of him, forcing his mid-back off the chair and placing him in a slanted position.

Roberts glanced down at the small protrusion at his waist and vowed to walk five miles every day. Make it six, he thought to himself.

"Very well, Mr. Gorman. Could you tell me what you know?"

"I don't know her name. I never know their names. They get on; they pay; they get off. Most times I never remember any of them. Once in a while, if somebody is real nice, I notice. I remembered a guy once who was having a heart attack . . ."

Jesus, this guy could keep me here a week, Roberts thought to himself. "Tell me about Mrs. Kidd."

"Oh, yeah, sure. She was really purty. That's how come I remember her. And another thing. I thought it was strange she was traveling at night, and with her kid, too. I thought to myself, they should be home in bed. Know what I mean?"

"Yes. Go on."

"Well, like I told the police . . . I mean, your people there in New Orleans, she got on at Alexandria. Her buyin' a ticket to St. Louis, I wasn't quite prepared for her to get off."

"Get off? I thought she went to St. Louis."

"No, sir. I told them fellers in New Orleans she bought a ticket for St. Louis. I didn't tell 'em she *went* to St. Louis." Raymond shook his head and rolled his eyes, as if the whole world was half nuts except for himself.

"But you just said she got off."

"She did. Right here in Little Rock."

Roberts scribbled notes to himself as his mind reeled into fast-forward motion. "And the boy was with her?"

"Yep. Cute little guy. Carryin' that WalMart bag. Bigger 'n he was."

Roberts only stared at Raymond.

"The bag."

"Oh."

"Guess now you'll be wantin' to talk to Jilly Bob."

"Excuse me?" Roberts stopped writing.

"Jilly Bob Perkins. The driver who picked her up here in Little Rock."

"She took another bus? Headed where?"

"Houston."

"Damn," Roberts muttered to himself under his breath. "Where can I find this . . ." He referred back to his notes. "Mr. Perkins?"

"Houston. Today he's in Houston. He'll be back here day after tomorrow."

Roberts carefully closed his notebook. He didn't want Raymond to know that he felt like a fool, chasing all over the countryside, when the answers he needed weren't in Little Rock at all. Why was it that he seemed to be the only person in his department who asked the right kind of questions? He started to rise and then sat back down again. He didn't want to be guilty of the same sin as his colleagues. "Raymond, before I go, is there anything else you could tell me about Susan Kidd? Did she ask any questions while on board your bus? Is there any detail I might have missed?"

"Let me think." Raymond tapped the side of his cheek with a chubby finger as his eyes scanned the dirty ceiling.

He was milking this moment of self-importance for all he could, Lieutenant Roberts knew. *I don't care if I have to sit here all day and night, if he gives me something to go on.*

"Did she say anything to you at all? Maybe ask about jobs or for directions of any kind?"

"No. Can't say she did. In fact, she was purty worn out. She and the boy slept mos' the way. I don't mind, you know. I don't have to have company to stay alert on the road. That's why the company keeps me on. I can stay awake and alert through anything. I drove four days straight through one time."

"That's admirable. But about Susan . . ."

"She never asked me nothin'. She never said a word."

Roberts couldn't hide his disappointment.

Raymond smiled briefly, thinking to cheer the investigator. "So, why don't you ask me the most important question?"

Roberts gazed quizzically at Raymond. "I asked you if there was anything else."

"But you didn't ask me where she got off." Raymond stretched his neck up out of his collar like a proud turkey.

God deliver me from morons who think I'm Perry Mason and Angela Lansbury rolled into one. "Okay, Raymond. Where did she get off?"

"Not in Houston." Raymond laughed and slapped his knee. "Ha! I bet you thought she was in Houston."

Roberts swallowed hard to keep his frustration in check. "Do you know where she did get off?"

"No, sir."

"Does Mr. Perkins?"

Raymond leaned conspiratorily closer to Lieutenant Roberts. "Jilly Bob . . . he's a bit tetched."

"Teched?"

Raymond tapped his forefinger to his temple. "Teched. In the head. He thinks he's gone up on one of them spaceships. Been with the aliens, he tells us. He's always predictin' stuff and seein' stuff that's gonna happen. A real spooky bastard, Jilly Bob is."

"What's all this got to do with Susan and Robbie Kidd?"

Raymond started laughing. He laughed long, hard, and rolling guffaws as he tried to relate the truth to Lieutenant Roberts. "Jilly Bob . . . he says . . . that Mrs. Kidd . . . that she just . . . disappeared!" Raymond threw his arms up into the air and made a huge circle with his hands. "Poof. Magicaboola. Bibbity, bobbity, boo."

Shit. Just my luck that my only leads are a prankster and a space freak. "Don't tell me: He thinks she went up on a spaceship."

"You got it."

Raymond was laughing so uproariously that Roberts didn't bother asking for directions to a telephone. He left the room believing he'd just developed a permanent case of claustro-phobia.

He went to the teller window, where an intelligent-looking young girl of college age with short dark hair and expensive wire-rimmed glasses was selling bus tickets. Roberts guessed she was a college student working here for the summer.

"Excuse me, miss. Where would I find a pay phone?"

"Over there." The young woman pointed to the left hall-way near a soft drink machine. "Do you have proper change? If not, I can make change for you."

"Thank you. I'm fine. But could you tell me the number of your Houston terminal? And perhaps the manager there. I need to speak with one of the drivers."

"You would want the office number and not the reserva-tions desk. That would be," she looked on a sheet of typed numbers underneath the glass top on her counter, "area code 713–555–7455."

"Thank you very much."

"You're welcome, sir."

Roberts dialed his precinct and asked for his assistant, Ser-geant Patterson, but Brian was gone for the day.

He placed a call to the Houston bus terminal and requested Jilly Bob Perkins. The woman on the other end of the line stated that he was out sick and not expected back for two days, when he would drive his route back to Little Rock.

Lieutenant Roberts thanked the woman and hung up the phone. Upon weighing his options, Roberts knew that Captain Michaud would tell him to fly back to New Orleans. How-ever, Captain Michaud didn't know Lieutenant Roberts had gone to Little Rock in the first place. Therefore, a quick flight to Houston to interview Jilly Bob Perkins could be just as easily overlooked.

He was certain the bus company would give him Jilly Bob's address. Roberts knew his interview would take less than an hour. If he handled it correctly, he could be back in

New Orleans by morning and his superior would be none the wiser.

Roberts picked up the phone again and placed a call to Southwest Airlines and made a reservation for the next flight to Houston. He ordered a cab to take him to the Little Rock airport.

Roberts no longer questioned the urgings of his intuition. He was too old and too wise to waste his time on inconsequentials. The one thing he did know was that when he had a feeling of being pushed toward some place or someone, it was always best he follow his instincts. It was when he didn't pay attention to his inner guides that he screwed up. He knew he needed to go to Houston and there he would find his answers. Roberts was confident that as soon as he spoke with Jilly Bob Perkins, he would uncover the truth about Susan Kidd.

It was important to him that he be the first one to find her.

Chapter Sixteen

New Orleans

Of all the places in the world, Jim Kidd knew most what to expect of the interior of a private detective's office. Because Jim had seen every suspense thriller Hollywood ever made he believed the filmmakers must have researched their subjects in order to accurately depict them on the screen.

The Canal Street address of Tate Rawlings, Private Investigator, had not given Jim a clue to the Old South, Greek Revival edifice he found. Next door to the red-brick-and-white columned newly built mansion was an asphalt parking lot rimmed with perfectly manicured boxwoods, colorful begonias, and heavy limbed oaks to provide shade. As Jim got out of his car, he was aware of three gardeners who clipped, pruned, mulched, and edged errant weeds and unwanted flora, creating an outdoors that was so meticulously clean, it appeared surreal.

The interior of the building was a further shock to Jim.

Where he'd been expecting grimy furniture, split Naugahyde chairs from the 1950s, and whirring desk fans, he found fabulous French and Italianate antique desks, chairs, crystal chandeliers, and plush Persian rugs to rival anything to be found on Royale Street. Instead of a blousy-looking receptionist who smoked cigarettes and chewed gum, he found a young, thin woman who wore her dark hair cut short, neat, and straight at the chin. She wore no makeup other than a light glossing of lipshine, and her clothes looked as if she'd just walked off the pages of a Ralph Lauren ad. She was as cooly elegant as she was proper. With a simple drop of her eyelids she made him feel three social classes beneath her.

"How do you do?" she asked with marked emphasis on her *oooos*, revealing her overstudied elocution lessons.

"Fine," Jim replied as he stood over the Louis XV desk, where she sat reviewing a leatherbound appointment book. "I'm here to see Tate."

The girl ran a perfectly manicured finger down her very full book. "Yes, James Kidd. You're a bit early and Mr. Rawlings is still in conference with another client. Would you care to be seated? I could get you some coffee or tea."

"Coffee would be fine."

She rose from her tapestry-upholstered Carlos V chair and went to an English sideboard located under the medieval tapestry of a hunting scene. She looked back to Jim and with her hand indicated a rosewood settee against the opposite wall, a few feet away from the circular staircase. "Please, have a seat, Mr. Kidd. I will serve you over there."

"Huh? Oh, yes." As Jim sat down he thought he'd never felt like such a social boob in his life. This woman had the ability to make Emily Post feel uncomfortable.

With flawless grace she handed him a cup of steaming French market café au lait, a monogrammed white linen napkin, and a sterling silver spoon. She placed a silver footed sugar bowl on the mahogany coffee table in front of him. She went back to her desk and began forwarding phone calls to other offices that Jim guessed were located on the second floor.

Jim reached for the sugar bowl. Geez, at least the coffee table was a reproduction.

Jim sipped the hot coffee and grew more nervous by the minute. This place must cost a fortune to run. Who pays for all this? he wondered. "You will, Bubba," he muttered to himself.

"Mr. Rawlings will see you now, Mr. Kidd."

Jim looked at the receptionist. "But . . . I didn't see anyone leave," he blurted.

The elegant woman raised her swanlike neck and smiled beneficently upon him, as if he were one of her royal subjects and, most likely, he thought, the court jester. "Our clients' privacy is of utmost importance to us, Mr. Kidd. You, too, may use the back entrance. There is a canopied walkway from a fenced parking area. No one need ever know you've employed us."

As Jim followed the woman down the main hall, he couldn't help feeling his money flowing out of his wallet already.

She tapped lightly on a paneled mahogany pocket door. "Mr. James Kidd is here to see you, sir."

"Come," was the answer.

She rolled back one of the pocket doors to reveal an enormous two-story library, complete with marble fireplace, parquet floors, and a rolling library steps. Jim could smell the new wood, but somehow the artisans who created this room had made it look as if it had been standing since the Civil War.

If the rest of Tate Rawlings, Private Investigator, had surprised Jim, the man himself was a double shock. Rawlings was no more than twenty-five years old, nattily dressed in expensive black wool slacks, white broadcloth cotton shirt, leather and tapestry suspenders, and an exceedingly conservative gray and burgundy tie. Tate's blond hair was more meticulously trimmed than the fancy gardens outside. He was about six foot tall, lean, with broad shoulders and perfectly chiseled facial features. He was a handsome man who looked as if he'd never dirtied his hands in his life, except to pick up a tennis ball. It amazed Jim that Tate's chosen profession was dealing in other people's personal muck.

"How do you do, Mr. Kidd?"

"Fine."

"It's such a pleasant day outdoors, it makes one rather annoyed that we must remain indoors to deal with business, does it not?"

"It does," Jim said, wondering if he'd answered correctly. Jim had thought Susan's parents were etiquette-obsessed, but this guy was ridiculous.

"Please, James, have a seat." Tate sat in an imposingly constructed burgundy leather wing chair.

"Jim. Thank you." Jim sat down across from Tate. As Jim glanced briefly around the room, he noticed that nothing was out of place. A huge bouquet of summer flowers rested on a coffee table, and each bloom looked as if it hadn't rested in the crystal-clear water less than five minutes. Jim pulled at his collar, as if his mounting bill was already strangling him.

"How may I be of service to you?"

"My wife left me and I want you to find her."

Tate's face was expressionless as he waited patiently for Jim to continue.

Why not? He's on the clock and it pays plenty. Jim hurried on. "Susan took Robbie, that's my son, with her. . . . It's been over a month now. I don't know where she is or why she left. But I want her back. The police seem to feel she might have been abducted. But they can't seem to get off their butts to do anything about it. That's why I'm here."

Tate placed his elbows on the arms of the chair and peered

at Jim over the tops of his steepled fingers. "You have been to the police, then?"

"Yes. Boy! What a thoroughly rotten experience that was."

"Why is that, James?"

"They acted like I had abducted Susan." Jim shook his head.

"Oh, I don't think they thought anything of the kind, James. You must understand that you were overwrought at the time, and sometimes our perception of certain situations is not all it should be."

"I hadn't thought of that."

Tate's smile was curiously enigmatic as he continued the interview. "In order for me to best serve you, James . . ."

"It's *Jim*," Jim interrupted.

"Yes, I beg your pardon, but to continue, you must realize that some of my questions might be a bit distasteful to us, but nevertheless, they are necessary. I'm afraid it's the nature of the business."

"I understand," Jim replied. "I . . . I didn't tell the police, because of the way they were treating me, but Susan and I have had a few arguments as of late."

"And?"

"Well, she's always nagging me a lot and I've had a lot of stress at work with this enormous Japanese deal I just closed." Jim glanced up at Tate, feeling increasingly uncomfortable in the pristine surroundings. Being studied by a man whose own life had a long time to go before he collected the first dust mote made Jim feel defensive.

"Excellent going, Jim. Was it a large commission?"

The hair on the back of Jim's neck stood on end. He could practically see the dollar signs in Tate's eyes. "It will be if everything goes right. Should take a year, though." Better cover myself, Jim thought.

"Good. Now please tell me about these arguments. I only

need this to help me with my investigation . . .''

Suddenly it was as if an alarm bell rang in Jim's head and the clanging was making him nuts. "I don't get this. What difference does it make *why* Susan left? She split. Period. End of discussion. She went somewhere. It's your job to find out where that somewhere is and tell me. *That* is what I'm paying you for,'' Jim growled as he flexed his fingers and then sat back in the chair. Jesus! What did he have to do to get some goddamn action out of people? He was paying Tate, wasn't he? Tate was his goddamn employee, wasn't he?

"I understand your concerns, Jim,'' Tate said with that unnerving aloofness that was beginning to drive Jim crazy. "This is simply a matter of lack of communication between us. You see, if Susan left because of a whim, or some secret desire to shop in Paris for a week or so, she will be back and there is little to concern ourselves about. If there was truly an abduction or foul play, that is entirely another matter. And, too, if Susan was unhappy, she might relocate to another town, but perhaps not far from here, and there's the chance that she might return. However, if Susan was abused, she would go underground, and we could spend the rest of my life and yours trying to find her and we never would.''

The truth caused Jim's mouth to dry up in an instant. He tried to talk, but his tongue felt swollen with his lies. "Underground?''

"She would change her name, her appearance. She would go far away, say California. She would blend with the masses. She would create a whole new life for herself and Robbie.''

"Susan couldn't do that.''

"Why not?''

"She's not that smart.''

Tate chuckled to himself, then cast a coldly brutal eye on Jim. "You're making that same mistake, Jim.''

"What's that?''

"Underestimating your wife. She is smart enough to have

not only left you without a trace, but she has successfully evaded the police for over a month. I'd say she was very smart, indeed.''

Jim looked away from Tate's brutally calculating stare.

"I need to know from you, Jim, which of my assessments most correctly fits your situation.''

Jim was hesitant to answer. "The last one.''

Tate nodded his head. "Then we know what we're up against.''

"You'll take the case?'' Jim was stunned that Tate with all his manners, would bring a woman back to her abusive husband.

"Of course.'' Tate stood and held out his hand to Jim. "Let me assure you that I will do all I can to bring your wife and son back to you. I have a nationwide network of investigators working for me. Some are former CIA, policewomen, and FBI agents, though they are not as effectual in their work as others. You will be amazed at our efficiency. In the meantime, did you bring the photographs we requested?''

"I have a folder in the car.''

"Good. Charleen will give you a brief questionnaire to fill out with basic descriptions, size, weight. That kind of thing. And she will set up your billing account for you. You can use the room at the right at the top of the stairs to finish the necessary paperwork while I see to my next client. In that room you'll also find soft drinks, coffee, and a full bar. In half an hour tea sandwiches will arrive from our caterer.''

"You think of everything.''

"We want you to be as comfortable as possible during this time of ordeal.''

"I appreciate that,'' Jim replied cordially as Tate walked him to the office door and rolled it back.

"I will have my people begin immediately. You rest easy, Jim; it won't take long to find your wife.''

"You don't think so?''

"We're very thorough and very good. We couldn't command the kind of business we do if we weren't the best, now could we?" Tate smiled again.

"I guess not."

Charleen came walking down the hall, nodded to Tate and turned to Jim. "If you'll please follow me, Mr. Kidd, we'll finish with your paperwork."

Jim turned back to Tate. "Thanks again."

"Thank you, Jim." Tate went back into the seclusion of his library.

Charleen took Jim upstairs and handed him four sheets of questions about his "missing persons" and then asked, "Which credit card did you wish to use today, Mr. Kidd?"

Jim was surprised. "I had planned to write a check."

"That would be fine, too. It's two thousand for the retainer and eight hundred a week thereafter until Mrs. Kidd is found."

Jim knew his bill would be stiff, but this was exorbitant. Maybe he should forget the whole damn thing. Maybe he should take the time off work and look for Susan himself. No, he couldn't do that. He'd lose his Japanese deal, and if that went through as it should, he could easily pay what Tate asked. Jim wanted to find Susan before the police did. If Susan told the police and her parents that he'd hit her, Bart Beaulieu would press charges against him. Jim would lose not only the Japanese deal but his job. He'd lose his position in New Orleans, such as it was.

No, he had to find Susan first and talk to her. He had to convince her to keep her mouth shut. He would promise her the moon if she'd put their past in the past where it belonged. Two thousand bucks was cheap when he thought about it.

"Visa," Jim said and went back to filling out the questionnaire.

*   *   *

Tate Rawlings picked up the telephone and summoned Charleen. She answered immediately.

"Yes, sir?"

"Please confirm my tennis match for this afternoon at four. Dinner with the Cloonans is scheduled for seven at Commander's Palace, I believe."

"That's correct, sir."

"Tell me, Charleen, do you think that Mr. Kidd saw Mr. Beaulieu leave through the rear entrance?"

"Oh, no, sir. I know he didn't because I had to explain the procedure to him."

"Very good. Mr. Beaulieu is an old friend of the family and I wouldn't want his personal business bandied about. Confidentiality is our stock in trade. And we certainly wouldn't want anyone to think there was a conflict of interest, now would we?"

"Oh, no, sir."

"One more thing, Charleen."

"Sir?"

"Tell Bob Franklin I've decided on the gold Jaguar convertible."

"Gold, sir?" Charleen's voice was filled with amazement.

"I thought it a bit showy, but upon consideration I think it still in good taste."

"By all means, sir." Charleen ended the conversation.

Tate Rawlings paid no attention to the twinge of greed that crept onto his shoulders. He spread another layer of polish over the corruption that had begun to cover his values and buzzed his secretary that he was ready for his next client.

Chapter Seventeen

Houston

Susan reached for a porcelain Lladro clown and felt a searing, shooting pain in her abdomen. She clutched at her stomach and when she did the Lladro went tumbling off the wooden shelf and crashed onto the highly polished saltilo tile floor below. Never having so much as chipped a plate in one of Merry Maids' clients' homes, Susan was the first to be shocked at the accident.

Micaela came running from the bathroom and Juanita raced in from the kitchen.

"What happened?"

The lady of the house, Vicki Bushman, rushed in from the terrace, where she was having lunch with two of her friends, looked at the broken porcelain, and said in a stunned, hushed voice, "My mother gave me that Lladro. It's the only one I have."

Susan watched the silvery blond woman as she bent and

166

reached for the broken fragments. It was evident that the piece had meant a great deal to Mrs. Bushman. Susan knew how she had felt leaving behind the momentos and family heirlooms her mother had given her. Susan's heart went out to the woman.

"I'm sorry. I'll replace it," Susan said, knowing words weren't enough apology and that she couldn't afford to reimburse the woman.

"You can't. . . ." Vicki stood holding the broken pieces and then turned around and started to leave.

Suddenly Susan felt another searing pain in her abdomen. It was as if someone had run her through with a sword. "Aaahhhh!" Susan screamed with a pain so intense, the room seemed to swirl beneath her. She lost her balance and reached for the shelf, but she was too late. She fell off the step stool.

"Star!" Micaela screamed and rushed to Susan just as she hit the tile floor.

"My God!" Vicki screamed and went to Susan's aid.

Susan was nearly unconscious from the intensity of the pain. She tried to speak but couldn't.

"I'll call an ambulance," Vicki said and headed for the telephone.

Susan thought she could hear Micaela's voice, but she wasn't sure. She floated in and out of consciousness and back and forth through time, until she was no longer aware of herself. She didn't know who she was or where she was.

At one moment she could hear Vicki's voice as she gave her address and directions to her house over the phone to the 911 operator on the other end of the line. The next moment she heard the doorbell and the sound of heavy footsteps around her.

"Bring the gurney while I finish taking her vitals," a man's voice said.

"I'll call the hospital and tell them we're bringing her in," a young man's voice answered. Then she heard the sound of his running footsteps.

Susan opened her eyes, but only long enough to see unfamiliar faces peering down at her. She felt the cool temperature of the tile beneath her, but not the texture of its bumps and ridges. It was as if she were floating. The world went black and then dawned again, now occupied with the unfamiliar faces of the paramedics.

She wanted to tell these people to find her son. She needed to tell Robbie herself what was happening, even if she wasn't quite certain what was wrong with her. Robbie's life had become filled with strangers lately. She was his only family. She was afraid that if Robbie heard the truth from a stranger, he would panic. She had to protect Robbie, not send him spinning into a whirlpool of fears.

"Rob . . ." she tried to say his name, but her body felt paralyzed.

One of the paramedics bent over her to listen to what she was saying, but Susan faded out of reality again.

"Ooowwwww!" she screamed when a young man with a stethescope around his neck pressed his fingers into her abdomen. She felt as if he'd shot her with a gun.

She didn't remember the two young men picking her up and placing her on a gurney. However, she was now being wheeled out the front door of the house into the sunshine. When the gurney bumped over the doorsill Susan screamed again.

There were tears in Micaela's eyes as she held Susan's hand. "I want to ride with her to the hospital."

"No way," came the response from the younger paramedic.

"I'll hang on the bumper all the way," Micaela threatened as she clung to the back bumper of the ambulance.

The younger paramedic called her bluff. "For her sake, just follow us in your car. Okay? You can't ride with her; you aren't family and you would get in the way if we had to go to work on her. Okay?''

''Okay.''

Susan drifted out of consciousness as they closed the doors to the ambulance and she lost sight of Micaela.

Susan instantly awoke as another pain stabbed her midsection. She tensed, clutched her stomach, and looked to the dark-haired young man who hovered over her. He pushed her black hair away from her face and touched her forehead tenderly.

''You're gonna be fine. Really. Just hang on,'' he said with a smile she'd only seen drawn on the faces of angels she'd seen in church.

Susan was afraid. Deathly afraid. She could never remember being seriously ill, and her lack of experience and knowledge about such things terrified her. Every muscle in her body tensed, which only increased the pain. Susan thought she'd never felt so lonely in her entire life.

Suddenly she wanted to see her mother's serene and beautiful face. She wanted to feel the touch of her mother's hand. She wanted to tell her mother that she was sorry for not calling her and sorry she felt she couldn't confide in her, but she didn't want to hurt her mother. Susan still didn't want to hurt her mother. She believed that if she could only hold her mother's hand, she would stay bound to earth somehow.

This must be what it's like to die, Susan thought. *This emptiness. This uncertain and immense vacuum I live in at this moment is all there is. There is no past and no future, only this moment.*

The intensity of the pain became torturous as the ambulance raced down the city streets. Susan would have screamed, but to do so meant she would have to breathe, and Susan was in too much pain for that.

At the Red Oak Hospital just off FM 1960 Susan was

wheeled into the emergency room, where more nurses prodded and poked, and a doctor examined her.

Susan was given a painkiller that allowed her to breathe again and return to more complete consciousness. She could hear Micaela's distinctive voice as she argued with a tall, gray-haired, robust-looking nurse.

"You can't move her. She just got here!" Micaela was nearly screaming.

"She has no insurance. We have to send her to Ben Taub. They have wonderful care there."

"She'll rot there! Everyone has heard stories about Ben Taub," Micaela retorted. "Can't you give her something to make her well and send her home?"

"I'm afraid not," the nurse said compassionately. "We don't know for certain, but the doctor thinks she has a ruptured ovary. She needs X rays, surgery. She's a charity case. She has to go to Ben Taub. I'm sorry, really, but those are the rules. There's nothing I can do." The nurse left the room.

Susan's mouth was desert dry, but she finally spoke Micaela's name.

"M . . . Micaela. What's she saying?"

Micaela rushed to her side and leaned over the metal guardrail on the bed.

"What's wrong with me?"

"They say it's your ovary. But they could be wrong. They haven't even taken X rays yet. So, it could be anything. Even my jalepeños from last night," Micaela joked, but concern furrowed deeply into her brow. She took Susan's hand. "I'll stay with you. I called Sandra and she sent over another crew to finish the house. She told me to tell you not to worry about anything. When you get well your job is waiting for you."

"And . . . the Lladro?"

"We're bonded, honey. The insurance will take care of it."

"Good," Susan said weakly as another wave of pain washed over her. "Tell me the rest."

Micaela lowered her voice to a whisper. "They're sending you to the charity hospital. I told you to buy the insurance Sandra offered."

"I couldn't, Micaela. I thought it was too risky. What if they found out ... my phony license and all ..." Susan blanched more from her fears this time than from the pain.

"Well, your way sure doesn't help," Micaela scolded her. Then she caringly patted Susan's hand. "Let's not worry yet. First you have to get well."

Susan thanked God for the friend she had found in Micaela.

Just then two paramedics walked into the room. "Star Kaiser?" the short one asked Susan.

"Yes."

"We have to drive you to town. It'll take us nearly an hour because the traffic is backed up on I-45. I'm going to put this oxygen mask back on you. We'll be as gentle as we can."

Susan pushed the mask away. "Wait!" She turned to Micaela with panic in her eyes. "Find Max. I want Max to be with me." Susan reached out to Micaela with desperation, digging her nails into Micaela's arm. "Tell him not to be scared, please. Nothing like this has ever happened to us. Promise me!"

Micaela nodded her head and touched Susan's cheek. "Don't worry about a thing. He'll be just fine, and if I have to smuggle him into your room myself, I'll make sure you see him. Okay?"

"Okay."

"I'll call Andie and have her drive Max to the hospital right away. And this time I *am* riding with you in that damn ambulance," Micaela said with fiery determination in her eyes.

Micaela turned to the paramedic with her hands placed defiantly on her hips. "She hasn't got any family here but her kid and me. Is there a problem with my going with her?"

"I guess not," the short, dark-haired paramedic said.

"Good. I've got to make a phone call for her and then we can leave."

The taller paramedic stepped in front of Micaela, bent underneath the gurney, and retrieved a belt that he flipped across Susan's rib cage to the other side. The short paramedic buckled the strap.

Susan winced as they struggled with the strap. Every movement sent another piercing jab of pain through her body.

"Take it easy with her, guys," Micaela blasted at the paramedics, who instantly agreed not to buckle the second strap. Satisfied that under her supervision Star would receive better care, she left the emergency room only long enough to call the apartment complex and talk to Andie.

Robbie inserted the videotape of *Aladdin* into the video cassette recorder and pushed PLAY. "The movie will be on in just a minute," he told the younger children sitting in a semicircle around him.

"Turn it up, Max. I can't hear it!" Mary, the red-haired six-year-old said.

"I want some juice!" Jamie, the four-year-old boy demanded of Robbie.

"Okay," Robbie said and handed the remote control to Mary. "You fix the volume while I get some juice for Jamie."

Mary grabbed the coveted remote control from Robbie and pressed the volume button a half dozen times. "I like it loud."

"That's too loud!" Jamie squealed with his hands covering his ears. Finally Mary relented and turned the volume to a normal decibel.

Robbie went to the cabinet where Toni kept the boxed juices. He grabbed a grape-flavored one, punched the pointed plastic straw through the tiny sipping hole on top, and handed it to Jamie. He was just about to sit down with the group when Andie walked into the room.

"Max?" Andie said.

Robbie turned around at the mention of his alias. Andie's face looked as if someone had painted it white. Her eyes were dark with the same kind of fear he'd seen in his mother's eyes the night they'd left home. His smile fell off his face as he walked toward her. "What's wrong?"

"It's your Mom, Max."

"Is she dead?" Robbie felt icy cold all over.

"No. But she's sick. She's in the hospital and she wants to see you."

Robbie looked at Andie as if she were crazy. His mother had never been sick. Why would she be sick now? And why would she have to go to the hospital? The only thing Robbie knew about hospitals was what he'd learned from sneaking peaks at the soap operas on television and from listening to his grandparents talk about their friends who were really, really old and died in hospitals. Robbie knew that if his mother was being taken to a hospital, she was going to die.

Robbie had believed since coming to Houston that he was the man of the house now, and that he was taking care of his mother. He was the oldest kid in day care. He took care of the little kids sometimes because they got scared when they didn't see their mothers all day. Robbie was looked up to by the little kids.

Suddenly Robbie felt as though he was a little baby again. He felt small and weak. He didn't know how he was supposed to act right now; he only knew that he was very, very scared.

I have to see her. I have to see my Mommy, Robbie thought as his mind blackened with fear.

Robbie didn't feel his tears when they first came to his eyes, but they were falling in profusion and he seemed surprised he could make them that fast.

Robbie kept trying to talk, but there was a burning lump

in his throat he'd never felt before. *I have to see my Mommy*.

He grabbed Andie's hand. "Will you take me there? I'm just a kid. . . . I can't get there by myself."

"I know, sweetheart," Andie replied, her own eyes swimming with tears. "I'll drive you."

Robbie looked up at her with a face filled with trust and gratitude. "I'm glad you're our friend, Andie. I need you."

Andie thought her heart would break for this little boy whom she had come to care for. He was struggling with himself, trying to act mature when she believed she could almost see his world shatter around him. "I'm glad I'm your friend, too, Max."

They walked swiftly to Andie's car, got in, and drove away from the complex.

Robbie tried desperately to see out the windshield, but his seat was low and the seat belt forced him back into the seat. He felt that if he could just see the road, he could help Andie drive faster, but the traffic was bumper-to-bumper. Robbie felt as if he were going to jump out of his skin. There had to be a way to get to his mother faster.

Robbie fought tears, wiped his nose on his T-shirt, and then gave up and put his face in his hands and cried.

Andie tried to comfort him the best she could. "She'll be okay, Robbie."

"If the cars would just drive instead of sitting still, then I could be with Mommy. Why won't they just *go?!*" He slammed his little fist against his open palm.

Like a miracle, the cars did move to a crawl. Within minutes they were up to speed. As they neared the 610 Loop Interchange they saw several police cars off to the side with four smashed cars and a red-and-white bus that was overturned in a ditch.

"Was . . . my mommy hurt in a car wreck?" Robbie's face was ashen as he turned to Andie.

"Oh, no, sweetheart. She got sick at work. Maybe it's just

a really bad flu or something. I'm sure it's nothing serious.''

As they drove, Robbie noticed that Andie's hands gripped the steering wheel so tightly, her knuckles were white. It was taking so long to get to the hospital, Robbie thought as he struggled to look out the window. Then he saw a hospital on the right that they passed up completely.

''Where do we have to go?'' Robbie asked, still looking back at the clean white-and-blue building now far in the distance.

''To the charity hospital.''

''Why there?''

''Because your mother doesn't have insurance or money. The doctors turned her away from the hospital close to us.''

Robbie was appalled at what Andie was telling him. That couldn't be true! Did things like that really happen to people? He remembered having a fever once so high that he'd gone to the emergency room at a clinic, and no one had turned him away. But that was before they left home. That was when they had money and his mother didn't have to work all the time. ''They shouldn't have turned Mommy away. Daddy has lots of money.''

''He does?'' Andie wasn't surprised at the information, but she was curious that after all these weeks this had been the first time Max had slipped.

Robbie suddenly realized he shouldn't have mentioned his father. He didn't want Andie to know how frightened he was, but he couldn't seem to stop the waves of tears that came to his eyes when he thought about his mother. Robbie felt as if his world had turned upside down. Nothing made sense to him. If his mother wasn't in a car accident, what could possibly have happened to her that she would need a hospital? She had seemed perfectly fine that morning before she went to work. They had shared his cereal and she had told him they might even go to a movie on the weekend. They talked about how hot the summer had become, and so they were making "cold plans."

"That's what we'll do, then. We'll go to an air-conditioned movie."

"And we'll eat ice cream and Popsicles for dinner," Robbie joked.

"On Sunday we can take the bus to the Galleria and go ice skating," Susan said, planting a kiss on his head.

"And we'll drink cherry Icies." Robbie laughed.

"Is that all you think about . . . eating?"

"Sure, Mom. I'm too young to think about jobs and girls and stuff."

"Girls?"

Robbie blushed, looked down at his cereal bowl, and shoved his spoon into his mouth.

"Do you have a girlfriend, Robbie?"

"Mary kinda likes me."

Susan nodded her head in approval. "She's the red-haired, pretty girl with the green eyes, isn't she?"

"Yeah. We get along pretty good."

Susan looked at her watch. "Omigosh, I've got to leave." She picked up her purse and waited until Robbie finished his cereal. "Tonight we'll make spaghetti and meatballs for supper. How will that be?"

"The best!" Robbie hugged his mother as they both walked out of the apartment for the day.

She poked her finger into his tummy. "No, you're the best."

Robbie imitated her gesture. "No, Mom, you're the best."

Robbie was glad that Andie was able to drive faster now that they were close to the city. He had to find out whether his mother was all right. He gripped the padded dash in front of him and strained against the seat belt. He could finally see the skyline of downtown Houston. Andie had told him it wasn't far to the Medical Center, but to Robbie it was still too far away.

Robbie tried to hide his fears, but he was so scared for his mother, he'd started shaking all over. He bit his lip so he wouldn't cry anymore. He kept silent as best he could because he knew that if he talked anymore he might say something wrong again. He didn't want Andie to know that he was uncertain whether he could take care of his mother by himself. He could make sandwiches and soup from the can, and if they had a microwave he could make even more things. But he didn't know anything about nursing. What kinds of medicine did she need? Would she have to be in a wheelchair? Self-doubt raced through Robbie.

The traffic thinned when they approached downtown, circled around the tall skyscrapers, and exited onto the Southwest Freeway. They took the Fannin exit off the freeway.

Robbie saw the Ben Taub Hospital sign before Andie did.

"There it is!" he shouted, anxiously pointing off to the left.

Andie pulled the car around to the Emergency Room parking lot. In his haste to see his mother, Robbie fumbled with the seat belt and became frustrated. "Get me outta here!" He was nearly on the verge of tears again.

"It's all right, Robbie. She's going to be fine. Really." Andie tried to reassure the small boy as she released his seat belt. Robbie scrambled out of the car in a flash.

The hospital was mayhem. Upon entering the front door, Andie and Robbie heard the buzz of hospital gossip. The victims of the accident they had seen on I-45 southbound had been brought here because it contained the best trauma units in the city. The worst injuries had already filled up the operating rooms, Robbie heard a passing nurse say to a young intern.

Robbie and Andie learned from the information desk near

the admitting office that Star Kaiser had been taken to the fourth floor, where she was awaiting surgery.

Robbie raced to the elevator and slammed his hand against the call button. "C'mon, Andie!" The elevator stopped on every floor on the way to them and did the same going back up again. Anxiously, Robbie wound the tail of his T-shirt around his forefinger and tapped his sneaker against tiled floor.

When the doors opened on the fourth floor Robbie had to push his way through a sea of adult-sized legs, hips, and arms. Andie followed directly behind him.

The reception area was filled with row upon row of metal chairs where families waited for their names to be called. The halls to both the left and right sides of the elevator area were lined with gurneys bearing injury victims and patients. Robbie saw a man of about thirty hugging himself and rocking back and forth on his chair. There were knife slashes up and down both his arms. Two chairs over sat a teenage boy with his arm in a makeshift sling, awaiting casting for his broken arm. A little girl looked at him from a far corner. There were what looked like round cigarette burn marks on her cheeks. The girl had an oddly vacant look in her eyes as she gave Robbie the once-over, then cooly dismissed him and went back to watching the television set high in a corner of the room.

A tall, thin nurse came into the area carrying an armful of files. She called out several names. "Jenkins. Samuels. Benton."

Three people stood and followed the nurse down another hall to the left.

Andie took Robbie's hand. "Stay close to me," she warned. Robbie noticed that Andie's hand was cold as ice. He knew she must be afraid, too.

Andie went up to a partitioned cubicle where a middle-aged nurse was sitting behind a window. "I'm here to see Mrs. Star Kaiser. They told me she was on this floor."

"Are you family?"

"No," Andie answered too quickly.

"Yes!" Robbie replied swiftly. "This is my Aunt Andie."

The nurse shot them both a scornful look. "Only family are allowed."

"I'm her son. I gotta see my mom. Now, please? We've come a long way. I gotta see her." Robbie placed his hands on the wall and leaned into the window, his chin just barely over the edge as he pleaded with the stone-faced woman.

The nurse filled her lungs with air and let out a sigh of exasperation. "All right, but only for five minutes."

Andie clucked her tongue at the woman's lack of compassion as she and Robbie followed the nurse to a ward room.

There were five gurneys in the room, all of them occupied. Robbie's eyes quickly shot around the room from right to left, and then he saw his mother in the last bed on the left.

Micaela saw them as soon as they entered the room.

"Thank God you're here, Max. She's been asking for you," Micaela said in a rush as she hugged Robbie. He kept his eyes glued on the still body in the gleaming metallic-looking bed. Everything looked just the way it did on television, he thought. Except that this was real. Very, very real.

Robbie had been in such a hurry to see his mother, but now that he was here he was afraid that if he touched her, spoke to her, whatever this evil force was that had brought his mother here might rub off on him, too.

"Mommy?" He walked cautiously toward the bed. The woman didn't move. He looked at the tubes running into her arm and the bag hanging overhead.

When Susan lifted her head a flash of pain seared through her body. She moaned and put her head back down.

Fear riddled Robbie's body when he recognized Susan. "Mommy! Mommy!"

Susan started crying. "My baby." She turned her head toward Robbie and raised her arm to him.

"Mommy." Robbie was crying as he rushed to Susan. The gurney was high, and he was still so small that he could barely reach up to her neck. All he could do was lay his head on her arm. "Mommy, I was so scared. I thought you might be dead."

This time Susan didn't mind the jostling of the bed. Robbie was with her. Somehow she had needed to see him in order to believe that she would survive this ordeal. She knew he was terrified, and she knew that she should be comforting him, she was the one who drew strength from him.

"Oh, no, darling. I'm just a little sick in my tummy. I would never leave you, Robbie." She tried to pull him closer. "I love you, Robbie," she whispered to him.

"I love you, Mommy." He looked up at her with mournful, frightened eyes. "What are they going to do to you? Do you have to stay here a long time? Why did Andie say you have to be at the charity hospital?"

Susan tried to smile. "So many questions," she said slowly with a thick tongue. The nurse had given her an injection that was intended to make her drowsy. "I'll be fine now that I know you're all right. I don't want you to be afraid. The doctor told me it would only take a couple of hours to fix my stomach and then I'll come home in three days."

"I don't like this place," he said, leaning closer to Susan.

"I don't either. That's why I'm coming home very soon. Micaela is going to let you sleep at her house while I'm here."

Robbie kissed Susan's forearm and then stroked it. "Don't be sick anymore after this, okay?"

"Okay." She winked sleepily at her son.

Just then the orderly walked into the ward. "Kaiser?"

"Over here," Micaela replied and motioned to the young black man.

"Time to put you back together," he joked as he unceremoniously pulled on the gurney and started down the hall.

Micaela walked after the gurney. "We'll stay here until you get back from Recovery, Star."

Robbie raced after the gurney. "I won't let them kick me out, Mommy. I'll be here. No matter what." Robbie didn't know what they were going to do to his mother, but a small voice from deep inside his heart told him that nothing bad would happen to his mother. His mother had told him once that the voice he heard was the voice of his guardian angel. Robbie had faith in his angel, and he found his courage again. Just as quickly as his fears had made him feel small, he now felt magically invincible.

Susan raised her hand and Robbie tried to touch her, but the gurney was moving too swiftly. Robbie watched as Susan was wheeled down the hall, her arm still waving in the air.

Robbie was left behind.

Chapter Eighteen

New Orleans

Annette Beaulieu dropped out of society. She refused dinner invitations, committee meetings, charity teas, and canceled her annual Fourth of July party and her Labor Day weekend trip to Sarasota Springs to visit the Dilworths at their condo. Annette did something completely out of character; she became introspective.

For over thirty days Annette had waited for the phone to ring, for a letter to arrive in the mail, for some kind of message from Susan. The silence had nearly sent her to the brink of insanity.

Normally prone to illness during times of crisis, Annette found to her own surprise that she didn't become ill during Susan's absence. Other than those first three days when she and Bart were interrogated by the police, Annette hadn't experienced another headache, upset stomach, or attack of nerves. Instead of retreating to her bed Annette had started asking questions of her friends—tough questions. Questions that normally would have shocked her now spilled from her lips. For a woman who had spent her life believing that nothing tawdry, nothing problematic would dare enter her enchanted paradise, Annette began searching for information with a vengeance. She was stunned at the turns her life was already taking.

For once in her life Annette wanted answers.

Annette stopped wringing her hands and pacing her bedroom. She picked up the telephone and called a psychiatrist whose name she had heard uttered with near reverence over many a bridge game with her women friends.

Dr. Alain Gilbert took less than an hour to show Annette that she, not Jim Kidd, was to blame for Susan's behavior.

"He struck her! I have never raised a hand to Susan."

"I never said you did," the tall, slender, dark-haired man with compassionate blue eyes said. "What I meant was that her relationship with Jim was one in which she placed herself under his control. Jim uses his fist to control Susan, but she had to be taught at home, by you or your husband, that being controlled was Susan's role in life. You didn't have to use physical abuse. Words would have done the trick."

Annette was so shocked she wanted to faint, but she didn't. How could this man gaze at her with such empathy while at the same time deliver such a sharp imprecation?

"I have done nothing but love and support my daughter all her life."

"I'm not doubting that for an instant, but during your therapy what I am hoping to accomplish with you is to remedy a sense of misdirection in some of your behaviors. For your sake and for Susan's I am hoping that you will have many self-revelations. It won't be easy. In fact, it will be difficult. This therapy will be the second most difficult act you will ever perform in your life."

"What was the first?"

"Making this appointment." He smiled compassionately as he rested his elbows on the arms of the chair in which he sat.

Annette noticed that he didn't take notes, nor did he even have a pad or pencil with him. She was glad about that, and silently thanked him for making her feel this comfortable. "So, it's downhill from here?"

He chortled his response. "I wouldn't go that far. It's just that I want you to be prepared for what is ahead. If you thought I would give you simplistic answers to your quite difficult questions, you were wrong. Therapy isn't a Band-Aid, but it is the path to a cure."

"But finding Susan is the cure."

"No, it's not," he retorted. "What will you do when she comes home? What will you do if you never find her? What if she does come home and goes back to her husband, which you so clearly have stated that you never want to happen? What will you do then?"

"But Susan knows that she always has a home with us. She knows that we will love her and take care of both her and Robbie."

"Obviously, Annette, she knows nothing of the kind. I can bet you my entire practice that Susan thinks you do not love her unconditionally. If she thought otherwise, Susan wouldn't have run away and you wouldn't be in this office."

Annette didn't like the way he kept throwing accusations at her. He kept trying to make her the villain in her relationship with Susan, and nothing could be further from the truth. "What are you trying to say? That I forced Susan to leave town and take off for God only knows where? Without a word to us?" Annette's nerves were being shattered and she felt perilously close to tears. She knew it was bad manners to cry in front of anyone. She knew this because her mother had scolded her often for her "tender sympathies."

Dr. Gilbert leaned forward and placed his elbows on his knees. His face was etched with sympathy. "Annette, please

184

listen to me. What I'm asking of you is to think about how you are going to handle your own life if Susan never comes home. You can't spend your life waiting by the phone. That kind of stress can only produce illness, and I do mean a major illness—cancer, heart disease. I don't want that for you.''

"I don't either." A huge tear hung on the edge of Annette's eyelash.

"You've already told me that you have a past pattern of getting sick at times like this. Lots of people do that—most people. That's why our hospitals are full. I just don't want you to be one of those people anymore.''

Annette pulled a tissue from the box sitting on the table next to the flowered love seat upon which she sat and dabbed at her eyes. "I don't either.''

"You can't control Susan's world anymore. You are her mother, not her keeper. Your only responsibility now is to yourself. I will help you understand what went wrong and why. Therapy will alter your perspective of your world. How you see yourself and everyone around you. You will see things you never saw before. Illusions will be dispelled and realities enhanced. It's going to be tough. You may agree with me at times. Other times, you may not. That's your choice. But if you choose to come back here again, Annette, nothing in your world will ever be the same.''

Annette Beaulieu had never been spoken to in the way Alain Gilbert spoke to her. He frightened her. He provoked her sensibilities. He was brash and incredibly intelligent. He made her think about every word she spoke, every thought she had. He had already changed her life. She wasn't sure if it was for the better.

What had once seemed simple suddenly was quite complex.

He gazed at her expectantly. "It will be a better world for you, Annette. That I can promise you.''

A tremenduous pressure began at the base of Annette's

neck; she felt as if her head were being crushed in a vise. It took all her energy to beat back the familiar waves of pain. "I . . . I'm not sure I have that much courage."

"I'm sure," he said resolutely with an encouraging smile.

Annette didn't want to be sick anymore. She was too young to be plagued with illness. She was just beginning to realize that there was a great deal about life that she knew nothing about. It was a frightening adventure she was about to undertake, but the alternative—the life of a near recluse—was all too familiar. When she'd re-examined the questions he'd asked her she hadn't known the answers. What would she do if Susan came home? Would she say the wrong things? Would she do something to push Susan away again? Annette didn't know what it was she'd done to make Susan leave her this time, and maybe once she understood that she would learn how to relate to her daughter in the future.

The thought of never seeing Susan again was unbearable.

"I want to love my daughter, not control her. I want to hold my grandson again," Annette finally said.

"Then I'll see you next week?"

"Yes," Annette replied with a kind of hope she had never felt before.

Chapter Nineteen

Lieutenant Roberts hadn't found Jilly Bob Perkins at the small hotel off the Southwest Freeway in Houston where he normally rented a room during his layovers, but instead tracked him down to the Westin Hotel in the Galleria.

Roberts parked his car in the lot of one of the most exclusive shopping malls in the United States and entered the plush hotel lobby. He went to the reservations desk and asked to speak to the manager.

A middle-aged woman dressed sharply in a black suit, her sandy hair pulled back in a French twist greeted Roberts with a smile.

He informed her of his identity, showed her his badge and credentials, and then asked whether Jilly Bob Perkins had registered with their hotel.

"I'm not at liberty to tell you which room he's in. Our guests rely on us to protect their privacy."

Roberts took out a handkerchief and wiped the perspiration from his balding head. "Well, I just thought I'd ask, this being a reputable hotel and all. I know he's here because the manager at the Day Lite Inn on the Southwest Freeway told me Mr. Perkins was forwarding all his calls over here.'' Roberts turned around and indicated the row of pay phones against the wall. ''Now, all I have to do is go over there to that phone booth, place a call to your hotel operator, ask to be put through to Mr. Perkins's room, and if he's there, he'll tell me his room number.''

''And if he isn't in, you've accomplished nothing.''

''Precisely right. Wasted my time. I don't want to do that. You see,'' Lieutenant Roberts looked at the woman's name tag, ''Ms. Arnold, I'm trying to find a missing woman and her seven-year-old son. Mr. Perkins was the bus driver who brought her to Houston. I was hoping he could help us find her. That's all. Mr. Perkins isn't in any kind of trouble. Your hotel isn't in jeopardy of bad publicity or shoot outs, or any of that kind of thing.''

Ms. Arnold breathed a visible sigh of relief. ''In that case, Lieutenant Roberts, perhaps we could bend the rules a bit.''

''I would be most appreciative.'' Roberts waited while the woman checked her computer log.

''He's in room six-twenty-two. The elevators are to your right.''

''Thank you very much,'' Roberts said graciously as he headed toward the bank of elevators.

Roberts entered the mirrored and polished brass elevator and rode to the sixth floor. He knocked lightly on the door marked 622. The door was opened almost immediately.

The pleasant-looking man with prematurely balding dark hair and an infectious grin presented his hand immediately to Lieutenant Roberts.

''Jilly Bob Perkins. Are you one of the reporters?''

Roberts was taken aback. ''Reporters?''

''From *People* or from *USA Today?* The local newpaper fellas have already left, so I know you aren't one of them,''

Jilly Bob said, hooking his thumbs in his suspenders.

"I'm here to ask questions, but I'm not from the press," Roberts started to explain. He was about to reach into his pocket for his badge, but Jilly Bob grabbed his arm and hauled him into the room.

"Well, don't be standin' out there in the hallway. C'mon in. Have a seat," Jilly Bob said jovially. "What can I get for you? Soda? Water? I had them bring me up plenty of ice. No liquor, though. I don't drink. Never have. Never will."

"A soda will be fine." Caught off guard by Jilly Bob's effusiveness, Roberts stole a few moments while Jilly Bob placed ice in a glass and poured a soft drink to take stock of the man who might be his only real hope of finding Susan and Robbie Kidd. Jilly Bob looked to be in his mid-to-late thirties. His features were sharp and angular, yet his mouth was full and friendly. He wasn't quite six foot tall, slender with athletic-looking shoulders and back. His clothes weren't expensive, but they'd been selected with a good eye and excellent taste. He looked more like a stockbroker than a bus driver.

Roberts accepted the glass and mentally discarded everything Raymond Gorman had told him about Jilly Bob Perkins.

"Thank you," Roberts said. "If you don't mind my asking, why are reporters coming to see you?"

"Because of the television special I'm on."

Roberts nearly choked on his soda. "You? When?"

"Tomorrow night," Jilly Bob answered proudly. "That's why I took this room. I don't have a place in town, but Houston is where the action is, as far as publicity goes. I can't believe how nice everyone has been to me. I thought they'd treat me like a nut case, the way everybody I work with does. But, you know," he scooted to the edge of his seat and looked Lieutenant Roberts square in the eye, "I think the time has come when people like me are more the norm than anyone had thought. The time is right."

Roberts leaned away from Jilly Bob. "You're talking about the aliens."

"Exactly." Jilly Bob stared at Lieutenant Roberts. "You need to watch the special; it will blow your mind. Since the time I was three I've been abducted by these silvery-looking people; in fact, they almost look like us, but not quite. Other abductees describe them as little, ugly gray people, but mine weren't. They never hurt me. They didn't poke, slice, or dice. They told me how their planet blew up due to a meteor shower that hit a series of their nuclear reactor plants. Some of them escaped into spaceships, and they've been waiting out there in our galaxy for the right time to colonize here on earth. They call themselves the Janos People." Jilly Bob suddenly realized that Roberts wasn't taking any notes. "Say, if you aren't a reporter, who are you?"

The lieutenant placed his drink on the table and reached for his badge. "Lieutenant Nathanial Roberts from New Orleans. I'm investigating a missing persons case—a young woman and her son. I was told by your co-worker, Raymond Gorman, that you drove the bus she took to Houston the night of June ninth." He pulled out a picture of Susan.

Jilly Bob frowned. "I thought you were a writer or something. Maybe a novelist. I heard that sometimes they crash these press conferences to get ideas. Aren't you a little old to be a cop?"

"You don't look like a bus driver, either, Mr. Perkins," Roberts bandied back.

"That's because I've only been doing this for a year. I got laid off at Compaq. I was a computer programmer for specialized businesses before that," Jilly Bob explained. "Raymond Gorman has been a thorn in my side since the day I started at the line. I think he's threatened by me."

"I see."

"The bus line is only temporary until I find something else. I suppose he told you I don't have a place to live and that I stay at a fleabag hotel on the Southwest Freeway all the time.''

"Something like that." Roberts took out a notepad and pen from his jacket pocket and began writing notes.

"I lost my house and my wife in 'eighty-seven during the crash . . . Wall Street crash. I've been saving every dime I can so that if I ever lose another job, I'll never have to go through this again. Of course, this room cost quite a bit, but I can afford it.''

Jilly Bob looked down at the photo. "It's so strange that you bring up this woman now.''

"Why is that?''

"Because I do remember her getting on the bus, and she had a little boy with her. Never having had any children, I don't key into them very well. So, I couldn't tell you much about him.''

"Here's a picture of Robbie." Roberts handed Jilly Bob a photograph.

"Cute kid. It was the strangest thing about her. She got on the bus, but she didn't get off. We made a stop in Nacogdoches, but I clearly remember her getting back on the bus. I think she vanished.''

"That's impossible.''

"No, it's not. People vanish for hours at a time every day. Every night. I have.''

"The aliens, right?''

"Exactly." Jilly Bob smiled at Lieutenant Robberts as if the older man knew precisely what he meant.

Roberts shook his head. "Susan Kidd disappeared all right, but not on a spaceship. Could you think about that night? Think about who else was on the bus? Did Robbie leave the bus alone?''

Jilly Bob rubbed his chin with his thumb and forefinger. "No, the little boy left with a woman. But she had very short black hair and was dressed like a rock star groupie.''

Roberts snapped his fingers. "Why didn't I think of that?"

Jilly Bob shook his head. "What are you talking about?"

"A disguise. There's a bathroom on your bus, isn't there?"

"Why, yes. Of course."

"Susan went to the bathroom, cut her hair, dyed it black, changed her clothes and—"

Jilly Bob looked crestfallen. "You mean she didn't vanish that night? She was on the bus all the time?"

"That's my guess."

"I'll be damned. Here all this time I thought she was another abductee."

Roberts reached for the photographs of Susan and Robbie. "No, she's just a person in trouble."

Jilly Bob Perkins peered deeply into the old man's face. "Is she a relative?"

"No. Just a case I'm working on."

"I realize you think I'm a bit wacko—aliens aren't exactly in the mainstream—but I want you to know that I wish you all the luck in the world finding Susan. She's not just another case to you. It's evident you care for her a great deal."

Roberts was uncomfortable talking about his emotions with a stranger. He stood quickly and started out of the room. "Good luck on your interviews, Mr. Perkins."

Jilly Bob Perkins extended his hand to Roberts. "It's time the word got out, Lieutenant. I'm just a vehicle for God's work."

"God? I thought we were talking about aliens."

"They're the same thing. Parts of the whole, Lieutenant."

Roberts couldn't get to the door fast enough. As he rode the elevator to the lobby and then walked out into the hot Houston sunshine, he thought about the intelligent man who had clearly lost a large portion of his brain. And yet that same lunatic had provided him with his best lead.

Susan was in Houston.